#thighgap
Published by Cemetery Gates Media
Binghamton, New York

ISBN: 9798818120188

My Dark Library #2

For more information about this book and other Cemetery Gates Media publications, visit us at:

cemeterygatesmedia.com
twitter.com/cemeterygatesm
instagram.com/cemeterygatesm

Cover Artist: Justin O'Neal
Cover Design: Carrion House

Title page illustration by Ryan Mills

For the angels.

"No blurb will be able to fully convey how great this book is. Chandler Morrison's voice is unique, stylish and powerful. Required reading for fans of Bret Easton Ellis, Tom Piccirilli or Chuck Palahniuk."

Brian Keene, Author of *Ghoul*

"*#thighgap* is a story of abyssal redemption. A frozen palace of beautiful and broken people. It's brutal and tragically sexy and doesn't shy away from any of its dark interiors."

Autumn Christian, Author of *Girl Like a Bomb*

"Morrison beautifully illustrates the brutality and horrific agony that accompanies diagnoses such as anorexia, bulimia, body dysmorphia, and other self-injurious, trauma-driven behaviors. The protagonist's journey of pain is presented with transparent and vicious honesty. *#thighgap* is a book of importance and a story that has long needed telling."

Marian Echevarria, Co-host of *Mothers of Mayhem*

"Swift. Vonnegut. Palahniuk. All authors who affected societal change through their satiric voices and social commentary. Now, in 2022, it is Morrison's voice that is added. *#thighgap* will leave the reader gutted while shining light on an overlooked and too often misunderstood illness."

Christina Pfeiffer, Co-host of *Mothers of Mayhem*

"Fast and dark, like a bitchier, pithier Bret Easton Ellis. Morrison has written a woman—and a dangerous, glamorous milieu—that we will see ourselves in whether we want to or not. Scratch the surface of this book and watch it ooze."

Lindsay Lerman, author of *I'm From Nowhere* and *What Are You*

4

"Stunning in every sense of the word, *#thighgap* is my new favourite novella. In this harrowing tale, Morrison delivers a devastatingly accurate portrayal of body dysmorphic disorder and spiralling psychosis. This depiction—along with the biting observations, droll dialogue and hideous caricatures that we've come to expect from Morrison's work—serves as a vital commentary on our aesthetic-obsessed society and perfectly captures the zeitgeist. Disturbing, dazzling and beyond beautiful, this is Chandler Morrison operating at his very finest. *#thighgap* is a book that will haunt you long after you've finished reading and is an important addition to the canon of eating disorder literature."

HLR, author of *History of Present Complaint*

"Since nobody writes as uncompromisingly as Chandler, it's no wonder he chose the coldest paths of the vapid and grotesque to tackle the brittle delusion of anorexia. Yet, with his portrayal of unlikable people in the eerily familiar metro-dystopias that spawn them, a character like Helen Troy is an astonishing trouble doll we find ourselves clinging to, like a death-grip on your last matchstick."

Gabriel Hart, author of *Fallout From Our Asphalt Hell*

"A cutting meditation on youth, beauty, and the price we pay for those very things. *#thighgap* opens a window into a very specific sort of hell, one filled with such grotesqueries even Hieronymous Bosch would stare, baffled, at the cavorting, self-made caricatures."

Brian Asman, Author of *Man, Fuck This House*

"I fucking love *#thighgap*, and I adore its protagonist; Helen Troy is a fully realized, honest character, and I respect and am inspired by her grind. She's my personal icon and North Star."

Gigi Levangie, author of *The Starter Wife* and *Been There, Married That*

"And in the lowest deep a lower deep,
Still threat'ning to devour me, opens wide,
To which the hell I suffer seems a heaven."
- John Milton, *Paradise Lost*

"The premonition of madness is complicated by the
fear of lucidity in madness, the fear of the moments of
return and reunion...one would welcome chaos if one
were not afraid of the lights in it."
- Emil Cioran

FOREWORD

Readers, do you ever have so much you want to say about a book that you sit down to write out your thoughts, but you really only manage to stare out the window?

Thinking about *#thighgap* and all there is to say about it had my brain in knots. I guess I can just start at the beginning.

Chandler's work leading up to *#thighgap* meets a specific expectation set by his readership to be extreme. I believe authors find success appealing to a particular demographic and there might be a temptation to continue selling work to those consistently showing up to buy it.

Once in a while, while I'm reading a book by an author with a very prominent brand or niche subgenre, I can hear the storytelling voice of another style just under the surface; wanting to break free; demanding to run in a totally different direction. This happened to me while I was reading Morrison's *Along the Path of Torment*, published by the Grindhouse Press imprint ATLATL. Even though *Along the Path of Torment* is extreme, it wasn't in the same vein as his big extreme horror title *Dead Inside*. There was something very *other* about Morrison's LA noir tone and styling that seemed to suit him so well. He writes so naturally in that voice–the narrative flows effortlessly. I told Chandler, that voice you're using in *Along the Path*, there's more of that inside you. You need to shake the extreme horror genre, even just for a season, to write the book you want to write.

Sometime later, *Human-Shaped Fiends*, Morrison's Splatter Western for Death's Head Press released, and there it was again—that *fucking* LA noir voice he used in the metanarrative.

Chandler agreed to write something for me. Something, unlike anything he's published before; leaving behind any expectation to continue delivering that jaw-dropping nastiness he's so good at and all his fans show up to receive.

So he did. It will be released soon from Stygian Sky Media and I love it. I can't wait for his readership to fall in love with this storytelling voice too.

But until then, we have *#thighgap* for My Dark Library.

A tragic, extremely forthright telling of a young woman's struggle with her addiction to thinness. Immediately upon getting invested in this story, I thought about the current body positivity movement and how I think there is this huge push for everyone to see themselves represented positively in media.

With the exception being: very thin people who are obviously struggling or have struggled with an eating disorder.

Which I find interesting. We fight so hard against toxic responses to bodies that are heavier than the average, but do we engage in that same fight against toxic responses to bodies that are thinner than the average?

"They need to eat a burger."

"They look like a clothes hanger, not a model."

"Put some meat on those bones!"

#thighgap gave me so much to think about. So much to process as I went on this dark journey with the protagonist, Helen Troy. Through her experiences, readers see Helen the way she sees herself. We see the way she sees others. The way she is treated by strangers, her peers, her co-workers, her therapist, love interests, friends, and ultimately, the weight of everyone's perceptions and expectations.

It's absolutely staggering and an extremely important point of view. I commend Chandler for his bravery and the intuition that was necessary, to tell the truth of this story. I hope it has the same effect on all of you as it had on me.

Sadie Hartmann
June 7th, 2022

CHAPTER 1 – THE LOOK

"God, you're so thin. It's perfect. You don't even look like a woman. You look like a little girl."

The movie director says this from the bed, his eyes watching me from behind the Vuarnet sunglasses he's yet to remove. He isn't wearing anything else. As I stand admiring my naked reflection in the full-length mirror on the other side of the bedroom, it occurs to me I should be disturbed by the appreciative way he'd said I look like a little girl. The disturbing nature of things is always occurring to me when it's too late. I don't remember when this started. I only know it hasn't always been like that.

The bedroom is dark. "The Look" by Roxette plays low on my stereo. The curtains move with the soft wind coming in from the open balcony door. I could go out to the balcony and see the glittering sprawl of Los Angeles stretching beneath me like a field of golden embers, but I don't feel like looking at it.

I turn away from my knife's-blade image in the mirror and go over to the bed, climbing on top of the director. His mouth has the bitter taste of cocaine when I kiss him. He smiles. Murmurs, "Tell me your name."

"You know my name."

"Mm. *Helen Troy.*" He says it with an affected lilt of mock reverence. "With a face to launch a thousand ships." His index finger traces along my jawline and down my neck, becoming a hand upon my meager breast. "That's not your real name."

I roll off him, taking my cigarettes from the nightstand and lighting one. "Leave it to a man to wait till after he fucks a girl to ask her real name." I don't even know his name. Logan Something, I think, but I'm not certain; he isn't famous enough to warrant remembering. One unpopular miniseries on Netflix and a handful of pretentious indie movies nobody saw.

"It didn't seem important before," the director says.

I blow smoke at the ceiling. "What makes it important now?"

He considers this. "I don't know. Nothing, I guess. It was just something I thought of."

I could tell him my real name. It wouldn't change anything. He'd probably forget it as soon as I told him. It's only a name. A sound you make with your throat. Nothing but a collected assortment of letters like any other one.

I know this. Rationally, I know this. And yet I also know it would feel like a betrayal. It would, in a sense, legitimize the girl I used to be. The girl I killed. This would, in turn, be an affront to the girl I am now. The one I've built. Whittled from the amorphous hunk of flesh that was my former self. It wouldn't be fair to the new girl. Not when she's given me so much, and she has. She's given me everything.

"My name is Helen Troy," I tell the director. "Whatever it was before doesn't matter."

He stares at me. The tiny underlined "V" at the top of each lens of his sunglasses somehow seems significant. "How old are you?" he asks.

"How old do you want me to be?" I'm twenty-four, but I tell most people I'm twenty; twenty-four sounds too close to thirty in the modeling world, and photographers will believe anything you tell them if you're pretty enough.

"You don't want me to answer that."

"Well, then, the truth will disappoint you."

"It so often does."

After he fucks me a second time, he asks me if I came. I lie and tell him I did because I don't want to deal with male insecurity right now. The truth about that would disappoint him, as well—I'm the only one who can make myself come.

Once he's gone, I return to the mirror. It is my altar. My cheekbones, my xylophone ribs, my flat stomach, my thigh gap—these are my sacraments. For so many years I hated the mirror. It showed me ugly, unbearable things. Now it is mostly a comfort. And when it's not, when it demands more from me, appeasing it is a simple matter. The sacrifices it requires are so trivial in comparison to its rewards.

It used to control me.

I'm in control now.

When I go into my master bathroom to take off my makeup and do my skincare routine, I notice a clear, viscous substance smeared on the bottom of the mirror. I drag two fingers across it and raise them to my face. It's thick and sticky, like mucus, though it smells of rubbing alcohol and bleach. Seeing it on the tips of my fingers, feeling it against my skin as its scent assaults my sinuses, I'm suddenly overcome with a cold panic I can't place. The slime seems portentous of something. An omen.

I tell myself I'm being ridiculous, that the director must have sneezed when he used the bathroom before he left. The chemical smell is probably from whatever his coke was cut with. I wipe the mirror off with a paper towel and wash my hands. The mucus gurgles down the drain, but the panic remains.

CHAPTER 2 – THE COLD PANIC

Colette Parker calls me on a Friday afternoon when I'm being costumed and made up for a photoshoot in which I'm supposed to be some kind of woodland elf thing. The makeup girl is currently affixing me with prosthetic elf ears, and the costume guy is preparing a set of bat wings I'm apparently going to be wearing for some reason. I learned early on not to question the artistic direction of these things.

"There's this party in the hills tonight," Colette is telling me. "Bitch, I'm telling you this right now, your ass better be there." My phone is lying on the vanity counter, set to speaker. The volume is too high, so her voice has a loud, tinny quality. I reach for the phone to adjust the volume, but the makeup girl snaps at me to stay still.

Colette is a columnist for a bunch of online fashion and lifestyle magazines. She wrote a couple novels and goes to more parties than anyone I know. She has the aesthetic of a 1920s flapper, with her bobbed hair (often adorned with luxurious wigs) and her long ivory cigarette holder and the loud, shimmering dresses with which she ornaments her tiny body. I can't remember how or when I met her, but she carries about her an air of celebrity not often associated with writers; she always seems to be everywhere, friendly with everyone, and in possession of the best coke in the city. I've tried to get her to share her hookup with me, but she always insists he's "not in the business of acquiring new clients at the moment."

"Who's going to be there?" I ask her.

She starts listing off names—mainly studio executives and TV producers, a few writers, and a handful of real estate moguls. When she mentions the name Jasper Price, I interrupt her and say, "Jasper is going?"

Jasper Price is a guy my age who's made an impressive fortune selling "afterlife cyber-spas" for the dead pets of gullible millionaires. He explained it to me once, or tried to; it has something to do with cryptocurrency and blockchains and—I'm not too sure on this piece—DNA samples. I was never able to discern if it's a deliberate con on Jasper's part, or if he actually believes these cats' and dogs' consciousnesses are somehow being uploaded into a digital day spa when they die. I've been sleeping with him on and off for a year and a half, but I was never able to get that kind of insight into his inner machinations. I suppose that's a large part of his appeal.

"Oh, shit, bitch, I totally forgot," Colette says. "Do you two still have that whole Ross-and-Rachel thing going on?"

I wince, and the makeup girl scolds me again; she's now gluing glittery fish scales to my face. "That's not exactly how I'd describe it," I say. "It's not that...earnest."

"Good. Only ugly people are earnest. Anyway, so, you'll come?"

"I guess." I don't know why she invites me to these things. I've never gotten the sense she likes me very much. Then again, I've never exactly felt liked by anyone in LA, nor can I say *I've* liked anyone out here to any sort of notable degree. For the most part, we all sort of politely tolerate each other. We'll sometimes feel things like envy or lust for one another, and other times those feelings will sour into suspicion or hate, but affection is something so elusive it's almost mythical. There was a time, I think, I knew what affection felt like. In my past life, when I was someone else. But the memory of it is so distant and formless that it's become intangible. I'm not certain I'd recognize it for what it was if I were to feel it now. I suppose this should make me feel sad, but there's only a vast emptiness that doesn't feel like anything.

"Be there at ten. And bitch, don't try to be cool and show up late like you usually do, because it's not that kind of scene."

"What kind of scene is it?"

"Just not that kind. Ciao, bellisima."

Later, after I've dressed and gotten ready, I chase some Tums with a swig of Pepto Bismol to quell the rumbling in my stomach. I don't like doing this—in general, I like the rumbling; I like to imagine it's the sound of my organs eating each other, reducing the mass of my body. It is, however, necessary to try to stifle it when around people, because people like to say things along the lines of, "It *sounds* like you need to *eat* something," and I don't like being cornered into discussions about food. I'd rather pretend food doesn't exist.

I also take a cocktail of Excedrin, ibuprofen, and Vicodin for my hunger headache, as well as a few Xanax for my nerves. After doing a line of coke in the bathroom, I put on my Jacques Marie Mage sunglasses, and that's when I notice it.

The slime.

It's coated around the bathroom doorknob, dripping in long, gooey threads into a pool on the floor. Had it been there earlier? If it had, why hadn't I noticed it? The cold panic returns, curtailed somewhat—only somewhat—by the drugs. I try to imagine who or what might have left it there. The only explanation I can think of is my cleaning lady, who was here earlier. It does smell like rubbing alcohol and bleach, so it must be some kind of cleaning solvent.

This, at least, is what I tell myself as I grimacingly clean up the mess with a paper towel, and I'm high enough to almost believe it. I do one more line of coke before leaving, and it succeeds in pushing the thoughts of the slime from the forefront of my mind. Still, in the Lyft on the way to the party, I know the panic is still there, reeking of chemicals, lingering in the recesses of my brain. Rattling against its cage. Struggling against its restraints. Shrieking muted cries into a black void.

CHAPTER 3 – CHASING DARKNESS

"You two were never good for each other," Summer Priestly is telling me at the party later when I ask her if she's seen Jasper. "If I were you, I'd try *not* to run into him tonight."

Summer—whom I somehow came to know through Colette—is a novelist and social media personality who presides over a Twitter cult of meme-slinging edgelords whose ideologies seem to teeter precipitously between anarchism and fascism. I was never clear on how so many thousands of them came to adopt her as their leader. I think it had something to do with an ongoing meme about coffee sizes. She always has an entourage of a few of them whenever I see her—usually young guys and girls dressed in black and wearing Ray-Bans or Oakleys. Three of them are with her tonight—all of them boys of about eighteen or nineteen—standing like bouncers at crossed-arm attention in a kind of phalanx behind her. She's reclined on a chaise longue out by the pool, smoking a cigarette, donned in a chic, one-piece black bathing suit and vintage Jean Paul Gaultier sunglasses. She's thin and beautiful, but not as thin and beautiful as I am, so I don't hate her.

"I'm not trying to run into him or not run into him," I say, lighting a cigarette of my own, shivering in the November night air. I wonder how Summer isn't cold, but it's not worth asking. "I was just wondering if you saw him."

"He's bad news," Summer says. "Not worth it."

"Yeah, he's a fed," says one of her acolytes.

"Total simp," says another.

"Not based at all," says the third.

"He's definitely not...a simp," I say, sort of confused. "And...a fed? What does that...even mean? How do you guys even know him?"

"Don't have to."

"It's obvious."

"We are everywhere."

"Um. Right." To Summer, I ask, "How do *you* know him?"

"Don't be a fed."

"We'll ask the questions around here."

"Your question is not based."

Summer snickers softly and says to the boys, "At ease, gentlemen. She's okay." She hits her cigarette and says to me, "We have, um...mutual friends." She snickers again. "I don't know him *that* well. Just well enough to know you and him don't make a lot of sense together. You're both too self-obsessed."

"I'm not self-obsessed," I say, but I can't make it sound convincing. I take a long drag from my cigarette. The rush of nicotine adds to my generalized lightheadedness, and I have to sit down on the chaise next to Summer's. "There's a...um...I'm just..." I trail off, losing the thread of the thought in the disorienting whir of my sudden dizziness. I shut my eyes. Breathe deeply.

"You okay?" Summer says, sounding amused.

"She's not used to criticism."

"Bougie bitches like that never are."

"Not based in the slightest."

"Listen," Summer says to me, "I get it. The whole chasing darkness thing. The need to see how far down you can go. Do what you have to do. Just don't go so deep you can't make it back to the surface."

"Darkness is a fed."

"Total simp."

"The surface is based."

I open my eyes, grateful for the dark lenses of my

sunglasses but less so for Summer's, whose eyes I wish I could see. I have an uncomfortable feeling she isn't talking about Jasper anymore. That her words of advice have more profundity than I'm willing to examine at the moment.

Slowly standing up, I tell her I'll see her later and then wander back inside the house, where the music is too loud, and everyone is dancing and drinking and eating. High-end hors d'oeuvres and fattening finger foods keep getting shoved into mouths and ground into desiccated paste by grinning jaws. Seeing other people eating always arouses juxtaposed sensations of disgust and superiority within me. These feelings play off each other. Feed each other. My hunger becomes a halo. It gives me wings which carry me above the mortals so dependent on their sickening sustenance. I can look down on them, a god, reproachful of the humans' inability to control their cravings. I am a pure, perfect being. Untouched, untouchable. I exist on another plane.

Someone snaps a photo of me as I aimlessly move through the crowd. For a second, I detect an overpowering aroma of rubbing alcohol and bleach, and the scent of it in my nostrils stokes the cold panic for reasons I can't place. I tell myself it's only someone's shitty perfume—probably fucking Moschino Fresh Couture—and, after I've advanced a few paces, the smell is gone.

I'm digging through coolers in the kitchen, looking for White Claw, when I feel a hand on my shoulder. Turning around, I'm pulled into a one-armed hug by Zelda Singer, my longest-held friend in LA. I met her in my other life, back when I was a pathetic, aspiring filmmaker. I don't like her all that much. She directs documentary films that piss off a lot of people but make a reasonable amount of money and impress the right institutions. There's a pretty, mean-looking blonde girl with her. They're both wearing sun-glasses from Selima Optique.

"Helen," Zelda says, "you're looking great." She gestures to the blonde girl and adds, "This is Ianthe. She's cool but she doesn't do drugs."

Confused, I say, "Is that...even a thing?"

"I knew Helen before she was hot," Zelda says to Ianthe. "She was *fat* when I met her."

A tiny, crumbling death happens inside me. I can feel my ribcage constricting around my heart.

"Oh, gross" says Ianthe, raising an eyebrow and looking me up and down. "I mean, I can't picture it, though. Glad you got it together. You have a very cocaine chic thing going on now. Is that how you did it? Coke? Me, I just don't eat."

I'm dizzy. I don't like conversations like this. I don't like to be reminded of what I was. "Um, yeah," I say, looking around for an escape route. "Like, I...you know, there was also, um...keto. And I did a lot of...um, Pilates."

Both of them nod knowingly. Zelda starts to say something else, but I tell her I need a cigarette and squeeze past her.

I exit out a side door into a small, circular courtyard populated with ferns and bonsai trees and a statue of a weeping angel, and that's where I find Jasper. He's alone, smoking a cigarette on a stone bench near the statue. A tumbler of something rests beside him. He looks up at my approach, the light of the surrounding tiki torches flashing in the lenses of his Bulgari sunglasses. The automatic glass door slides shut behind me, sealing off the sound of the music and plunging us into silence.

"Helen," he says, not standing. He picks up his drink and raises the glass to me before taking a sip. "I didn't know you were going to be here."

"Colette invited me." I walk over and sit beside him, putting a cigarette in my mouth. My hands are shaking—I'm still rattled from the conversation with Zelda. Jasper lights the cigarette for me with a Cartier lighter. Hunching my shoulders against the cold, wanting to curl up into myself, I ask him if he's seen her.

"Colette? No. I don't think she's here. There's another party in Bel Air I'm going to later. That's probably where she is."

"Oh. She...didn't invite me to that one."

"You can come with me if you want."

"No, thank you, I...don't think so. I'm kind of...tired." This isn't a lie. I never have enough energy to be out for more than a few hours at a time. The coke helps, but it doesn't stop the protesting in my joints, or the pleas of my ever-atrophying muscles. I've come to love the weakness and its always-present aches, aches which are only temporarily alleviated by the painkillers. It's all a reminder of how unnatural my lifestyle is, that I'm defying my body's needs in order to be something more than human. Something better.

"You're always tired," Jasper says. "You just need to do more coke."

"I don't think that's it. I mean, I do a pretty, you know, reasonable amount of coke. I...think." An awkward pause passes between us, and then I say, "Jasper. Where have you been? I haven't seen you in...it feels like it's been a long time."

He takes another sip of his drink, hits his cigarette. "I've been around. I didn't go anywhere. I mean, work has been busy, as always. That's the great thing about pets— they're always dying. But you can text me, like, whenever."

I could, but that's not enough. *He* has to text *me*. He has to want me. Otherwise, there's no real point. I'm not sure if there's much of a point either way.

Glancing at his Breitling wristwatch, he stands and says, "I have to get going. Hit me up."

"I will," I tell him, hoping it's a lie but knowing there's a possibility I'll break down in the midst of a depressive episode of loneliness and longing, craving validation.

When he's gone, the scent of bleach and rubbing alcohol returns with such force I think for a moment I'm going to faint. I become aware of a sound I can only describe as *oozing*. A periodic, successive squishing noise like pus being squeezed from a lesion. Realizing it's coming from the statue, I stand and approach it, noticing it's actually a fountain—water is seeping from the angel's eyes and trickling down its body into a circular pool at its feet. Except...*trickling* isn't quite the right word because the water is moving too slowly. Its texture is off, too—it's too shiny, too slick.

Kneeling at the edge of the small pool, I dip my fingers into the water, only to be confronted with the nauseating understanding that it *isn't* water.

It's mucus.

CHAPTER 4 – BEAUTIFUL EROSION

It was in middle school people started calling me the slug. I'd always been fat, but I don't remember being fully, viscerally aware of it until sixth grade. Sixth grade was when my classmates—friend and foe alike—began to say things.

Are you sure you should have that second slice of pizza?

Jesus, bitch, do you ever stop eating?

How do you do your hair in the morning without throwing up when you look in the mirror?

And Jessi Vathek—captain of the cheer team, and the one who coined the slug moniker: *No way I'm walking behind her—I don't want to slip on her slug trail.* Jessi's insults stung the worst—not because they were the cruelest, though they often were, but because I idolized her. I wanted to be her. She was a perfect image of flawless, natural beauty.

I wish I'd had the fortitude to do something about it earlier. I should have started restricting at a much younger age than I did. I tried, but I never had the gumption to commit. My mom always filled the refrigerator and the pantry with everything I liked. It was right there in front of me all the time. Taunting me. I couldn't ignore it. I'd tell myself I wasn't going to eat any more Twinkies. No more strawberry shortcake rolls or Oreos. I'd make these vows at school after someone said something about my weight, and sometimes, I'd make it all the way through dinner and up to bedtime without giving in to my desire for garbage food. But then I'd be lying in bed, staring at the ceiling, *obsessing.* No matter how full my stomach was from dinner, it would twist and growl and insist on its fallacious emptiness. And so, inevitably, I'd end up in the kitchen after my parents had gone to sleep, and I'd gorge myself on snacks. Many times, I'd cry while I ate, looking at the thin bodies of my classmates in the sexy pictures they posted on Instagram. They with their cropped tops and thigh gaps and jutting collarbones. I'd read the comments boys left—drooling faces and heart-eye emojis and processions of little fire icons. These same boys hardly even looked at me in school, and when they did, it was with disgust.

Nobody wants to fuck a slug.

People don't even *pity* slugs. The only emotion a slug elicits is revulsion. A slug is something you want to slither away to wither and die somewhere out of sight.

I tried my hand at cutting as a means of punishing myself for my lack of resolve, but even that venture was pathetic and halfhearted. I could never summon the courage to use any type of blade, so I used the broken back of the battery compartment from a TV remote, dragging its jagged plastic edge along my inner thighs and the soft, flabby flesh hanging from my upper arms. These wounds were nothing more than scrapes which bled little and healed quickly and never scarred. I'm grateful now, of course, for the lack of scarring, but when I look back at that time, I'm embarrassed that I couldn't even commit to legitimate self-harm.

It wasn't until I was nineteen that I finally reached a point where I was too sick of myself to continue living the way I was. I made up my mind to kill the slug. I'd been living in Los Angeles for about a year, having come here to pursue some vague, half-formed "dream" of being a film-maker—something which now seems so nebulous and incomprehensible. Around that time, the short-lived body positivity movement was still a thing, or at least making the pretense of being one. Society never subscribed to that the way they pretended to. It was just another way for

24

thin, middle-aged women to pat themselves on the back for their pretense of inclusivity. The thing is, no one ever stopped being disgusted by fat people. Men still didn't want to fuck them. It was nothing more than one more lie to hide the ugly truth—that skinny is Good and fat is Evil.

I think what made me different from other fat girls was that I never disagreed with this truth, or even resented it. I *knew* being thin was the ideal. Even if the world *would* have accepted me for the slug I was—a theoretical impossibility, for all of everyone's posturing—I would have hated all of them for it. I never had any misconceptions about what beauty is. But I told myself—with bleating, misguided desperation—that there was more to life than beauty, and I could still do the things I wanted to do and go the places I wanted to go without being beautiful. Plenty of ugly people, I rationalized, were happy.

It was in Los Angeles, feebly attempting to navigate the entertainment industry, that I realized I was wrong. Ugly people *aren't* happy. The ones who claim to be are either lying, or they're too stupid and lazy to know there's something better.

At first, getting thin was only about being taken seriously among the other people in the industry. It was about fitting in. I saw how they looked at me. Saw the reflection of the slug in their eyes. I don't know what specifically gave me the resolve I'd never had as a kid. The cigarettes and cocaine—two habits I'd taken up as another means of fitting in—aided in my cause. It made skipping meals easier. It turned hunger into an afterthought. And through these chemicals, I discovered another high. One more natural. Cheaper. Easier to obtain.

I found that not eating was far more intoxicating than anything brought on by sugar, carbs, or fat. The longer, in fact, I went without eating, the higher I felt. It made me into a god. Seated me upon a pedestal I'd before thought unreachable. I'd never known control before; tasting it for the first time was better than any food I'd ever put in my mouth.

Better still were people's reactions to the weight loss. As the pounds fell off, I could feel everyone beginning to look at me in a new light. I never wearied of the double-takes, the "God, honey, whatever you're doing, it's working." And as time wore on, the double takes length-ened into lingering stares of appreciation, even lust. The blobby fat melted away to reveal something elegant. Something beautiful.

I'd never known I had beauty in me. I had always assumed I'd make an average-looking-at-best thin person. When the soft, doughy curves of my body sharpened into hard, graceful lines which came together to form a delicate creature of heart-fluttering allure, the revelation of my own magnificence was an awakening. I became obsessed with it. I honed and perfected it. Everything in my life shifted to accommodate my newfound need to achieve the utmost aesthetic splendor.

My caloric content kept decreasing until it dropped below 1,000; I currently fluctuate between 400 and 800. I discovered the miracles of intermittent fasting, starting with the 16:8 schedule before extending it to a 20:4 schedule, and oftentimes only eating once a day. There are times I'll go days without eating, but I've kept those stretches to a minimum recently. I weigh myself between six and fourteen times a day. I'm usually happy with the number, and when I'm not, I restrict until I am. I'm not a huge fan of purging, but it's a good tool to keep in my arsenal for times when I accidentally lose control and eat too much.

About a year ago, I flew home to Villa Vida, Ohio, for my five-year high school reunion. I'd not kept in touch with any of my classmates; the only reason I went was to show off my new body. My sparkling beauty. It was, for the most part, a resounding triumph. My former tormentors exclaimed over how gorgeous I was. They tried to act like we were old friends, feigning amicability, but I could see the hateful jealousy in their eyes. They only proclaimed their admiration for my transformation in a failed attempt to disguise their sickened envy. Many of them had become bloated and gross, settling into dull lives with high school sweethearts and popping out kids like it was their mission in life. It wasn't merely my beauty they despised—I'd escaped from the interminable mediocrity of smalltown life in the Midwest, and I'd *thrived*. I can't imagine how pathetic this must have made them feel. They with their dead-end jobs and dead-end spouses and dead-end kids in their dead-end neighborhoods.

Jessi Vathek was there, but she didn't join in the masked extolling of my reinvention. She hung around the drinks tables at the edges of the darkened gymnasium, the whirling disco lights occasionally lighting up her pouting face.

She confronted me in the bathroom toward the end of the night as I was checking my makeup and getting ready to leave. I turned away from the mirror and saw her there, standing in the doorway, scowling.

"My God," she said, shaking her head. "You were gross in high school, but...wow. You've really gone in the other direction and come all the way back around. You can't actually think you look *good*, being that thin. It's appalling. You look like a dog's chew toy."

I took off my Louis Vuitton sunglasses and looked her up and down. Unlike the other girls, she hadn't changed at all. She looked exactly like I remembered she did in high school. She was even wearing the same Miu Miu dress she'd worn to senior Homecoming. The one that I'd spent the rest of the year imagining myself in, if only I could be thinner.

What *had* changed was my perception of her. I could see her now. *Really* see her. What I saw wasn't so impressive. There were bunched-up pouches of fat beneath her bra. Her face lacked definition. Her thighs pressed together. Her ass was too big.

She'd never been hot. Not hot like I'm hot. She was decidedly average, and average is just another word for fat.

"What's so funny?" Jessi asked, sneering.

I put a hand to my mouth, realizing I'd started laughing. "I'm sorry," I said. "But...*you* are. *You're* funny. This must be hard for you. The school fatty is now thinner and hotter than you ever were. And that's...very funny to me."

The color fled from her face. "I...What? Come on. You can't—"

"Make sure you have someone put a 'wet floor' sign outside the bathroom," I told her. "You wouldn't want someone to slip on your slug trail."

I pushed past her, feeling exalted. She wanted to be me. They all wanted to be me.

They'd do exactly what I do, if only they could.

If only they had the stomach for it.

CHAPTER 5 – ADVENT OF THE SLUG

I can't handle it when I'm not the thinnest and most beautiful girl in the room. It arouses a frenzied panic in me that seethes like deafening static and drowns everything out. Reason, rationality, logic...these things are meaningless. They slip through my fingers right when I think I have a hold on them. It never makes any difference that I know I'm being unreasonable, irrational, illogical. When the death spiral of cold panic sets in, it will not be sated without some form of sacrifice.

Today, the panic comes at a shoot downtown for Celine, or YSL, or maybe Dior. I can't remember, and it doesn't matter. What matters is the girl in the dressing room, the girl among all the other girls, the girl who stands out. The girl who isn't me. I'm the one who's supposed to stand out. That's what I've worked for. What I've built through my steadfast commitment to erosion. I've gotten used to my presence making everyone else irrelevant, part of the scenery. Objects. So much plastic.

But.

This girl.

This girl has complicated the narrative. She's thrown everything into disarray.

I've been the second-best-looking girl on three separate occasions since my transformation, and the third-best twice. I remember where I was each time, what I was wearing, whom I was with...the time of the day, the lighting, how the air smelled, what I'd eaten in the last twenty-four hours. These times hang on a wall in a dark, shameful corridor in my memory, captured in digital frames, playing on a constant loop.

Those other times were bad, but they were manageable. I was able to recover from them with disciplined restriction and a few methods of what some would call "self-harm." But this time...this time, something is different. Something about this girl's ethereal flawlessness, her perfect proportions, her symmetry—it's too much. It makes me not enough, and in such a way that I'm suddenly, profoundly certain I'll *never* be enough. That, no matter what, I will never look as good as she does, and that because of this, everything is a waste.

She's standing there in a lace bra and panties that don't adorn her so much as *she* adorns *them*. It's as though these garments exist only to be worn by her, and without her they'd blink from existence. Her feet in their stilettoed pumps are small and graceful, lacking any of the inherent impropriety feet so often have; my own feet are my worst feature. And her hair, vibrantly hued a natural honey-gold, has such loud, luscious volume it makes me want to hide mine beneath a bathing cap.

More than any of this, it's her thinness which cuts deepest. Her body is like the edge of parchment. Being that skinny, she should look emaciated. Sick. Grotesque. It shouldn't work, but it does. She could glide over snow and leave its purity intact. And all the while, she'd look like a dream. Something too sacred for human eyes. A gift the world never deserved.

My name at once feels like a farce. *Helen Troy, with a face to launch a thousand ships*. No ships would launch for me. No men would die for me. Not when they could die for a girl like this.

She catches me staring. The cruel, treacherous planes of her faultless face point in my direction. One perfectly sculpted eyebrow raises just so. "What," she says. Flat, uninflected. The subtlety of the venom in her voice makes it all the more toxic. Like I'm not even worth real hostility. I realize she's younger than I am, too—eighteen, nineteen at the oldest. Her body is the knife, her age the salt.

"Nothing," I murmur, even though it's everything. I spin on my heel and bolt for the bathroom, locking the door and swallowing gulps of air. I need a Xanax, but I was foggy with Valium when I left this morning and forgot my to-go pillbox on the counter.

Something in the mirror at my periphery catches my eye. A shape that takes up too much space. I turn toward my reflection and have to clap a hand over my mouth to keep from screaming.

It's me, but it's not. It's the me I left behind. The me I killed. Fat, dowdy, pale. No makeup, bad haircut. Flesh overflowing everywhere. An amorphous disgrace, lumpy and misshapen. Her skin is coated with clear, shiny mucus. There are two bumps on her forehead, one above each eyebrow. They're too large and contusive to be mere blemishes. Like something is growing beneath the skin. Fighting to emerge.

The fat girl leans forward, and for a second, I think she's going to come out of the mirror, but she stays on her side. Pressed against an invisible barrier. She's grinning at me. Her teeth are smeared with something dark that I first think is dirt, until I realize it's chocolate.

"You're dead," I whisper. "I killed you. I starved you into nothingness."

She shakes her head slowly, still grinning that awful, chocolate-flecked smile. There's a pathetic hunger in her eyes, childlike and desperate. "You're wrong about that," she says. "I've been right here all along." She touches a sausage-shaped finger to the monstrous mound of her left breast. "I'm inside you. We're the same. You can starve and count calories and puke all you want. You can do all the coke in the world. Smoke all the cigarettes. You can do whatever you feel you have to do, but you'll never be rid of me. You'll always look like this on the inside. And sooner or later, I'll get back out." She presses a meaty palm to the invisible barrier. "You're a thief. You stole my place in the world. You've had your fun with it. But you can't keep it." Her hand closes into a fist that she raps against the barrier.

The mirror shudders. She pounds her other fist against the barrier. She keeps pounding until the mirror rattles from the wall and shatters against the sink. Shards of glass skitter across the linoleum floor. I have a sudden urge to pick one of them up and drag it across my throat.

Fighting back stunned, confused tears, I exit the restroom and bump into another model waiting outside. "Um, don't go in there," I tell her. "I was...throwing up. It...smells. I would...um, I'd use the men's room if I were you."

She gives me a knowing look bordering on compassion and starts to walk away. When she stops and turns back to me, I think she's going to say something about the noise from the shattered mirror, but instead she says, "Is someone else in there? It sounded like you were talking to someone."

"That's, um...that's the sound my throat makes when I'm gagging."

She shrugs and turns away, keeps walking.

The shoot is basically a disaster. I can't concentrate, and the photographer has to keep repeating his instructions to me. He gets annoyed. The other girls get annoyed. Everyone is annoyed. All I can think about is the perfect girl, but I can't look at her. I feel as though everything will collapse if I look at her. Everything which, just this morning, seemed so stable. The mirror was my ally. The fat girl, the old me—the *slug*—she robbed me of that. I want to kill her all over again, and not even just because she's fat. *She stole my mirror.* She called me a thief, but *she's* the thief. Thieves have no place in a capitalist society and should be put to death.

She doesn't know whom she's dealing with.

I'm *not* her.

I killed her once. I'll kill her again.

CHAPTER 6 – AN APPETITE FOR MISERY

A blackout brought on by the Xanax I copped from one of the other models—I didn't want to wait until I got home to my stash—culminates in a mountain of garbage food. Two burgers and two large fries from In-N-Out; mozzarella sticks, jalapeño poppers, and a large vanilla shake from Arby's; a Wendy's chicken sandwich; a dozen Hansen's cupcakes; four packages of Haribo gummy bears, a family-size bag of Cool Ranch Doritos, pretzels glazed in white chocolate, Sour Skittles, two oily slices of pepperoni pizza, and a hotdog, all from 7-Eleven. I come out of the blackout with the food spread out on a beach towel in my living room. Shredded fragments of grease-soaked wrappers are everywhere. Potato chip crumbs and candy are scattered amid the refuse like viscera. Most of the calorie-laden shit is only half-consumed; it seems I'd take a few huge bites and then move on to something else. My face, hands and arms are sticky with grease and frosting, ketchup and sugar, sauce and lukewarm cheese.

The horror I feel while gazing upon this tragedy of lapsed will is a sweeping force that cuts down my whole being. The rage rattles and shrieks within my skull. I try to scream but nothing comes out.

Running to the bathroom, I'm greeted again by the slug in the mirror, only now, she's even fatter. Fatter than I ever was even at my most disgusting. She's not even a person, and not just in the way that fat people aren't really people. She's an obese fucking *worm*, some kind of humanoid parody of that gargantuan slug in *Star Wars*.

Her mouth is a wide, toothy abyss, and from it come the words, "*Yes, bitch. Give in to me. Feed me. Don't stop feeding me.*"

I howl at her, feeling tears cutting through the food entrails caked on my face, and throw myself over the toilet. As the slug screams in protest from the mirror, I shove my fingers as far down my throat as they'll go. The puke comes out in a spigot, rushing over my hand, spattering the rim and tank of the toilet, splashing into the bowl. It keeps coming in violent gushes, spewing from my mouth and nose. Chunks of it get stuck in my teeth. I'm sobbing, which makes the acidic burn in my throat and sinuses all the more painful.

When it's over, I collapse back against the wall, coughing and gagging. The tears won't stop. I stay like that for a long time, my knees pulled to my chest, hating myself with an overwhelming magnitude I don't know how to compartmentalize.

After I don't know how long, I realize the slug in the mirror has ceased her admonishing cries. I get up and go over to the mirror, expecting to see her standing there, her mealy pink skin gone scarlet with indignation. In her place, however, is someone else. Some*thing* else.

A corpse.

My reflection is a corpse, naked and steeped in the advanced stages of decomposition.

Her skin, shrink-wrapped around her skeletal frame, is a greenish gray that almost edges into blue. The scant hair on her scalp hangs in frayed, tangled knots. The lips are split and chapped, and the nose is gone. Clusters of maggots wriggle in open lesions dotting her rotting flesh; I can hear the wet sounds of their squirming. A thin layer of fine hair is growing all over her body. Only the eyes show signs of life, haunted and luminous, seeming to glow from deep within the pitted caverns of their sockets.

"No," I whisper, trying and failing to blink the image away. "That's not me."

"Not yet," the corpse girl says, flashing a glimpse of

her shriveled black tongue and her chipped gray teeth. She has the voice of one of those devices they give to people after they have throat cancer. "Not yet, but soon. And that's okay. That's good. This is beauty. This is perfection."

It takes a lot of energy to shuffle from the bathroom and through my apartment to the bedroom, where I crawl into bed, shivering and clutching my phone. In an effort to make myself feel better, I open a web browser and start shopping. The first thing I do is buy eight pairs of designer sunglasses—two from Persol, one from Oliver Peoples, three from Jacques Marie Mage (my go-to brand), and two from LGR. For shoes, I go to Brunello Cucinelli, Walter Steiger, Chanel, Manolo Blahnik, Christian Louboutin, Jimmy Choo. Three purses from Louis Vuitton, two from Gucci. Last, I buy a bunch of dresses and lingerie—Celine, Dolce & Gabbana, Saint Laurent, Miu Miu, Halston, Dior, La Perla. Each one I add to my cart brings a jolt of dopamine; the slug could never have fit into any of them. The slug shopped at Target and the GAP.

It's not just about the sizes; the price tags give me a flood of warmth and well-being not unlike an opiate high. Seeing the four- and five-digit totals when I press "CON-FIRM PURCHASE" is like snorting a thick line of Oxycontin. I wasn't technically poor growing up, but I wasn't well-off, either. I've since come to the understanding that not being well-off is just a milder and more polite version of being poor. It's only been about four years since I started making real money, the kind of money that makes you look at everything differently, but it's still hard for me to imagine there was a time when I couldn't buy whatever I wanted.

Helen Troy gave me this. Her beauty and her body have brought me wealth beyond the slug's wildest fantasies. Without Helen, I'd be nothing. I'd be less than nothing. I *was* less than nothing.

Back when the slug was still alive and in control, Zelda told me once that I was never going to get anywhere in life looking like I did. In the throes of my delusion, I told her that beauty isn't everything. "Beauty is the only commodity that matters," she told me in response. It had seemed, at the time, like such a shallow and reductive worldview. It's easy to be dismissive of statements like that before you've been paid seventy-five grand for someone to take your picture for three hours. You see your face on billboards, magazine covers, social media ads with millions of views—that kind of thing rearranges your entire perception of the world, of yourself.

It's not something you can relinquish. You have to hold on to it no matter the cost.

I had no idea my grip on it was so tenuous.

You never realize how fragile you are until you're already in pieces.

CHAPTER 7 – RESHAPING REALITY

My therapist is a forty-ish guy named Hal who wears a lot of baroque suits from Versace and never takes his Cary Grant sunglasses off. He has an office in a Beverly Hills high-rise off Robertson and says things like "far out" and "no way" in response to what I tell him, usually while he's scrolling Instagram on his phone. I see him twice a month and pay him $400 a session.

I've just finished confessing to my food meltdown. It feels somehow less real having spoken it aloud. If it weren't so vivid, I could pretend I'd made it up. I make up a lot of things I tell him, commingling lies with truths until the two become vaguely indistinguishable. That's why I keep coming here, I guess. It's in this room I can reshape reality into something sensible.

"Hal," I say in the silence that follows my confession. "Are you listening?" I haven't told him about the slug in the mirror, or the corpse girl. That would be crossing a line.

Hal clicks off his phone screen and sets it on his lap. "Yeah, babe, for sure. That all sounds really wild."

"What do you think I should do?"

He thinks for a second, steepling his fingers and pursing his lips, his head bobbing in a slow nod. "I think," he says, "you should just chill out. Take it easy, you know? Relax." He grins. I think his teeth are capped—they're too white, too straight. He's a pretty decent looking guy even though he's basically geriatric. The work he's had done is subtle to the point of being hardly noticeable. His dark hair had flecks of gray at the temples one time, but I've never seen them since so he must have it dyed.

"I lost control," I say. "It's been years since I completely lost control like that. All that food, all those calories." I look out the floor-to-ceiling window, down at the trundling traffic a hundred or so feet below. A light raining is falling. Streaks of it slide down the glass like tears.

"I mean, you threw it all up, though, right?" Hal says. "So, like, what's the big deal? Crisis averted. You look great. You look slammin'. You're a smokeshow, babe."

"But your body still retains a bunch of the calories. And worse—if it happened once, it could happen again."

"You're always worrying about whether some shit is going to happen or not happen. Just fucking cool it, will you? I don't know why you're always coming in here all hella keyed-up. How much blow did you do this morning? Be honest."

"I...don't think I did any," I say, trying to remember. "But, I mean, look, the point is...something has, you know, changed. Something's different. I saw that girl at the photoshoot and—"

"What girl?"

"The perfect one. With the perfect face and the super skinny body and the great hair. The one who set all this off."

"Oh, right, that one. Got it, go on."

He has no idea what I'm talking about, but it doesn't matter. "I saw her," I continue, "and it totally threw me off. I saw her and I knew I'd never be her. So, it's like my brain just said, 'Well, if you can't be her, you're doomed to be the slug, so there's no use fighting it.' And then I *didn't* fight it. For a couple hours, I didn't fight it at all. The slug took over."

"And the slug is...?"

"Me." I flinch, hastily amending, "I mean, *not* me. Not the *current* me. But the old me. The fat me."

Hal leans back in his chair, looking exasperated. "Helen, I don't know what to tell you. You're not fat

38

anymore. You're hot now. Just stay that way, and don't get fat. It's really pretty simple. And hey, if you *do* happen to slip up and end up binging again, just do what you did this time and puke it out. There are actually some studies that were done recently about the health benefits of binging and purging on occasion. I haven't read them, but the titles sounded promising."

"It's not just that," I say, my thoughts turning to the corpse girl. "There's this other element, and—"

"Of course there's another element," Hal says, sighing and returning to Instagram.

"What I'm worried about all of a sudden is, how long can I keep this up? I've been doing it for years. I can't even remember the last time I had my period. I haven't been to the doctor in I don't know how long because I guess I've been sort of afraid of what they'll tell me. But...what if I'm, you know...killing myself with my behavior? I never really gave that notion much thought before, but now I *am* thinking about it, and I'm realizing that I don't want to die. But it feels like the only alternative is to become the slug again, and I can't do that. I *can't*. I don't want to die, but I'd choose death before I'd choose the slug. I'd choose death every time." It occurs to me that I'm crying, which both surprises and frustrates me. I don't know when the tears started, and I hate the feeling of them on my face. Taking off my Fendi sunglasses, I grab a handful of tissues from the box on the table beside the couch and swipe them across my eyes and cheeks.

Hal looks back up from his phone. Seeing my tears, he takes a deep breath and, setting his phone on his desk, runs a hand through his hair. "Listen, babe, don't cry. Here's the thing." He takes another breath and rubs his palms against his thighs. His face becomes deadly serious. "I'm doing a set at the Hollywood Improv tonight. It would mean a lot to me if you came. It's been, God, I don't know, at least a few months since I've been onstage, so it would be hella chill to have a friendly face in the audience."

"You're doing...a set? What does that...even mean?"

"You know, comedy. It's a standup routine. Just

something I do for fun now and then, but if I'm being honest, I do think I have the potential to really make it big. You have to come, you'll love it. I actually have a few jokes about you."

"You have...jokes about me? I feel like maybe that's...kind of...fucked up." Even as I say this, I'm not totally sure. Maybe it's normal. I've never had any other therapist, so I don't know where the boundaries are supposed to be.

"Oh, relax. I won't actually use your name if you're going to be all weird about it. There's this one I wrote last week, though—*total* banger—and it's about how you—"

An alarm on his phone starts beeping. He glances at it, slides his thumb across the screen to silence it. "Well, shit, looks like that's time. Anyway, see you tonight?"

"I'll...think about it."

"Far out, babe. Until then, think about what I said. Hang loose. Stay chill. Be breezy."

"Yeah," I say, standing up. When I get to the elevator, I realize I'm still crying.

CHAPTER 8 – SILENT UNDOING

O ver the course of the next week, I start eating more than usual. Not an obscene amount. Nothing crazy—typically between 900 and 1,200 calories a day. Still, it's too much. I don't know why this started—this sudden inability to keep my hunger in check, to stave it off. Something must have happened after the binge. A wire must have been tripped. A circuit shorted. It awakened something. I can no longer go more than fourteen hours without eating, and when I finally give in, it's harder to stop. There was one day I exceeded 1,400 calories, but when I tried to throw it up, all I could do was dry heave.

Wherever I go, I see the slug—in mirrors, reflected in windows, staring out at me from the lenses of people's sunglasses. She keeps getting fatter and more grotesque, more slug-like. The smell of bleach and rubbing alcohol never goes away. I see mucus everywhere. It drips from seemingly everything, collecting in noxious puddles.

Even with my tragically increased caloric intake, I'm hungry all the time. I can't stop thinking about food. My stomach growls and gurgles with insistent petulance. There seems to be an inflated number of restaurant advertisements all across the city, and with them, a proportionally higher quantity of beauty advertisements. One night, when I'm shivering in the back seat of a Lyft with a Wendy's salad growing soggy in its paper bag, I see the perfect girl on a billboard above Sunset. It's some sort of makeup advertisement. Her perfect face is huge and luminous, flashing a subtle, somewhat condescending smirk. Beneath her visage is the caption, *MAKE YOURSELF FLAWLESS.*

My shivers become more violent. I ask the driver to turn the heat up, and he has to thumb down the volume on the radio—which is playing an endless procession of Christmas songs—to ask me to repeat myself. I tell him it doesn't matter.

At home, I sob as I eat half the salad, hating myself more with each bite. This is not the way to MAKE YOURSELF FLAWLESS. This is the way of the slug.

When I go to the kitchen to throw away the remnants of the salad, I find that my garbage can is nearly over-flowing with mucus.

CHAPTER 9 – MUTUAL FRIENDS

Jasper calls me one evening after the sun has set, and I resent the way my heart jumps when I see his name on my phone screen. I let it ring four times before answering, the anxious anticipation building in my chest.

"Hey," he says in a way that sounds bored and tired and kind of strung out, but I guess that's how he always sounds. "Did you need something?"

I sit on the edge of my bed, balling a handful of the comforter into my fist. "Did I...need something? Like, when?"

I hear him light a cigarette. A drag. A pause. An exhalation. "I don't know. You texted me."

"I...did? Or, um...that was...that was days ago." I don't actually remember texting him. I must have taken too much Xanax one night recently.

"Yeah," he says. "I mean. I guess."

Squeezing the fistful of blanket, I say, "Okay. Well, um. I just wanted to see what you were doing."

Another exhalation. I can picture the smoke rushing from his parted lips. Can almost smell it. "I don't remember what I was doing."

"Right, well. It's...not important. Um. What are you doing...tonight? Do you want to come over?" I keep my voice tempered, trying not to sound desperate.

"Can't. My friend Calliope is singing at El Cid. I told her I'd go."

"Calliope Laing?"

He pauses again, for longer this time. "Yeah," he says,

dragging the word out. "Do you know her?"

"Like, not personally, no. But some of her songs come on my Spotify sometimes." I squeeze the blanket so tightly my knuckles crack. "How do *you* know her?"

"I can't imagine you listening to Calliope Laing. I always figured you listened to a lot of, like, I don't know. Hawthorne Heights, or whatever."

"I don't listen to Hawthorne Heights," I say, probably a little too quickly. "But you didn't answer my question." My acrylic fingernails puncture the blanket.

"Like, you know. We have...mutual friends. Listen." He takes a breath. "Do you want to come? She's pretty good live. Her recorded stuff sounds much better, but. I don't know. That's how it goes."

I let out the breath I now realize I'd been holding. "Yeah," I say, making an effort to sound casual. "Yeah, I'll come. I like her stuff."

"Wild. I didn't think anyone really knew who she was. She's not very popular. I mean, I guess she does okay, but I think most of her income is from writing songs for other people. And I think there's also, you know. Family money. She's not famous, or anything. She's kind of, I don't know. Niche."

"Well, I like her. And I really don't listen to Hawthorne Heights." I release the punctured comforter from my grip. "Do you want to pick me up?"

"I mean, not really. Where are you?"

"At home."

"Yeah, no, definitely not. I'm not driving twenty minutes to West Hollywood and then turning around to drive back here to Silver Lake. That's insane."

"No, yeah, that makes sense."

"Just meet me there at, like, nine."

When he hangs up, something cold and aching and broken inside me lets out a low whimper.

Later, I have difficulty doing my makeup because the slug is in the mirror. "Get out of here," I shriek at her, fighting back tears at the thought of having to see Jasper

44

with botched makeup, but all she does is shriek back at me. I have to resort to essentially putting the makeup on her fat face, struggling to match it with mine because the contours and planes are all wrong. The foundation clashes badly with her pale, blotchy skin. The sheen of slime turns it into a muddy soup.

When it's done, I stand staring at her absurdly painted face, and hope that my own face is even. "I killed you," I scream at her. "This isn't your life anymore. This is my life, and you can't have it back."

In case my eye makeup is off, I select a pair of gigantic Celine sunglasses that obscure a large portion of my face. After doing some coke, I take a handful of pills—Xanax, Norco, and Ativan—and leave my apartment. As I'm walking down the hall toward the elevator, I keep thinking I hear someone behind me, but there's never anyone there when I turn around.

CHAPTER 10 – TRAGIC POSTER GIRL

I get to El Cid right as Jasper is walking to the entrance. He turns toward me at my approach, his face expressionless. He's wearing a Brioni suit and Renauld sunglasses, and I hate him for how good he looks. I hate myself for wanting him.

He stares at me for a few silent moments, and I wait for him to say something about my makeup. Instead, he says, "You came. Whoa. I didn't actually think you...would."

The broken thing inside me recoils. "Why...wouldn't I? You invited me, and...and I said I'd...meet you here?"

"Well, I mean, yeah. But, like, you know. People say things. They don't always mean them. They usually don't mean them."

I don't know if he's trying to say that he didn't mean it when he invited me, or if he thought I didn't mean it when I said I'd come. I don't want to know.

Calliope has already started singing when we get inside. There aren't many people. We sit at a vacant booth, and a waitress brings us glasses of water. Jasper orders a gin and tonic. I tell the waitress I'll stick with the water.

I turn my attention to Calliope, who stands illuminated on the stage. Her long black hair has a lustrous sheen that gives it a tint of gunmetal blue beneath the beacon of the spotlight. Listening to her, I decide Jasper was wrong—she actually sounds better live. The melancholic longing in her voice has an added edge of desperation. She's quite pretty, too, if a little old and somewhat run-down. She must be at least thirty, and maybe even a few years past that. Her thighs and arms and stomach are kind of bloated, and there's a washed-out haggardness to her features. She probably drinks too much. She'd be stunning if she laid off the liquor and lost ten pounds. No, I decide, raising my sunglasses and squinting at her. Make that fifteen. Still, she has an old-fashioned beauty that shimmers through. Gently worn vintage.

She sings three songs. Jasper is on his phone the whole time, scrolling, absently sipping his drink. From the reflection in his sunglasses, I can see he's on Instagram. Not tapping anything. Just scrolling.

The sparse crowd scattered around the dark room applauds politely when the set is over. Calliope gives a little bow and a weak smile before being helped down from the stage—she's short, barely five feet, if that—and then she comes over to our booth and slides in next to Jasper.

Setting his phone on the table, Jasper says, "Hey. That was totally great."

"Really," I say, "You're wonderful. You have such talent."

She bats her eyes and flashes a sheepish smile. "Oh, well. Thank you. That's kind." Reaching her small hand across the table, she says, "I'm Calli." After I shake her hand and reciprocate the introduction, she adds, "You look amazing. You're so beautiful."

Part of me says, *I know.*

Another part of me screams, *Then why don't I feel beautiful? Why do I feel like a disgusting slug? Why can't I stop thinking about the 960 calories I consumed today?*

"Thanks," I tell her, glancing at Jasper. He doesn't seem to be paying attention. "So, um. You're based here in LA?"

Her face darkens. "Yes. Unfortunately. But I keep thinking about leaving. More and more, lately. I've been here fifteen years and I don't know if I can stand it any longer. It's so awful."

I feel my eyebrow lifting before I can subdue it. "Really? I don't think so. I mean, where would you even go? There isn't anywhere else. Like, I guess there's New York, yeah. But it's too cold to live there."

The waitress brings Calliope a glass of red wine, and Calliope knowingly addresses her by her name when she thanks her. Something happens in Calliope's eyes when they fix upon the glass. A frenzied ecstasy accompanied by a vast, desolate anguish. She shuts her eyes when she takes the first sip, and the corners of her scarlet mouth pull slightly upward into the hint of a small smile that somehow seems tortured. When she sets the glass down, she looks at me with a hard levelness in her eyes and says, "There isn't anywhere else? You don't actually think that, do you?"

I shift in my seat and take a sip of my water. "What I mean is this is the only place that matters," I say. "It's the center of the culture. Everything is here."

Leaning back, gripping her wineglass, she says, "What is it you do, Helen?"

"I'm a model."

The short laugh with which she responds has a subtle note of cruelty in it. "A model. Yes. That makes sense."

"Why does it...make sense?" *Because I'm beautiful. Tell me I'm beautiful again. Just keep saying it over and over and don't say anything else.*

"Look at you." That clipped laughter again, more perceptibly malicious now. "You're a stereotype. You're a walking embodiment of the city and all its false charms and promises."

I flinch. "They're not false."

"No, you wouldn't think so, would you? You've bought into the lie, and it's made you one of its tragic poster girls."

My eyes move again to Jasper, hoping he'll defend me, but he still isn't paying attention. Calliope sips her wine, her eyes alight with warm hate. I blink, disoriented. She'd been so pleasant at first. Seemed so kind. I don't know what set her off. "I'm sorry," I say. "I think maybe we—"

"Sorry? You're not sorry. Not for anything. You cash

the checks, don't you? You reap all the benefits. Those of us with actual *talent* toil and struggle for basically *nothing*, and people like *you* bat your eyes and the whole town rolls out the red carpet for you. You don't know what real disappointment is. You don't know failure. You *definitely* don't know what it's like to suffer."

"You don't know that. You don't know anything about me."

"Please. I've met you a hundred different times. Different versions of you, with slightly different faces, but basically the same. You think you're special because you're pretty, and because you're *so fucking thin*. Give me a break. Anybody can be thin."

"Then why aren't they," I say. "Why aren't you."

Calliope's eyes widen and her mouth drops open. She touches a hand to her cheek as if I'd struck her there.

"What's wrong?" I ask her, infusing my voice with treacly sweetness. "Has no one told you this before? That you're fat? You must know. You can't look in the mirror and not see it. Girls like you, you want all the same privileges as girls like me, but you don't want to do any of the work. Girls like me earned it. You haven't earned anything."

She opens her mouth to say something, and then closes it again. When she raises her glass to her lips and drains the rest of its contents, I note with satisfaction that her hand is shaking.

"Come on," I say. "You come at me with these cutting jabs about the whole essence of who I am, and then you crumple when I tell you that you're fat? If you're going to start a fight like that, have thicker skin. Shouldn't be difficult for someone of your size."

"Fuck you," she says meekly.

"Ooh, good one. Why don't you have another drink, honey. I think you've lost this round."

Turning to Jasper, Calliope says, "I'd like to leave. Let's get out of here." She touches her fingers to the collar of his shirt.

50

Looking up from his phone, Jasper says, "Um. Already? Did I...miss something?"

"Let's just get out of here," Calliope says again, hooding her eyes suggestively.

"Uh, yeah. Cool." He glances at me as he procures his wallet and lays two twenties on the table. "I guess we're taking off," he says to me. "Have a drink on me if you feel like it. I think there's enough there. I'd leave you with more, but you know I hate carrying cash so that's all I've got on me."

I blink at him, dumbfounded. How could he be leaving with *her* when *I'm* right here? *I'm* the beautiful one. *I'm* the skinny one. This bitch doesn't even have a thigh gap.

As they're leaving, Calliope says to me with a blazing fury in her eyes, "Helen, it was *so* delightful meeting you." And then she leans down and whispers, "Beauty isn't everything, cunt."

"It's the only commodity that matters," I murmur, but they're already walking away.

CHAPTER 11 – THE ANGELS OF EDTWT

At home, feeling particularly disgusting from the sting of Jasper's rejection, I resolve to retake control. I've been out of control for too long. Eating too many calories. This, I reason, is largely—if not entirely—to blame for tonight's embarrassing tragedy. The perfect girl took my life away, opened it up to the infiltration of the slug and the corpse girl. I need to take it back.

For thinspiration, I seek out the soothing delights of Eating Disorder Twitter. It's been months since I've perused the posts here, and the familiar hashtags— #thinspo, #bonsepo, #meanspo, #thighgap, #edtwt, #proana, #anamia, #bodycheck—are a comfort. These girls—my angels—are the unsung poets of the world. I don't even have to hate them for their extreme skinniness, because—in addition to the detached distance provided by the internet—I'm not in competition with any of them. The angels are my sisters. I feel a kinship with them I've never felt with anyone else. Their revelatory beauty is not an irritant, as it would be if I knew them in real life, but a salve.

@kagome_thinlife hasn't posted anything in over two months, which is unusual. I wonder idly if she's dead. @skinnypilled77 has reached her goal weight of ninety pounds and has thus moved the goal post to eighty-two. @msrexia_is_fasting gained four pounds and started cutting again. @shadowlimbs keeps posting an artfully decorated picture every few hours with "reasons not to eat" scrawled in delicate cursive. The reasons are:

1. You will be fat if you eat today. Just put it off one more day.
2. Skinny people fit everywhere.
3. Only fat people are attracted to fat people.
4. Food is not more important than happiness.
5. If you can name one reason to be fat, I'll name a million and one to be thin.
6. Thin people look beautiful in every kind of clothing.
7. Saying "no thanks" to food is saying "yes please" to thin.
8. YOU DON'T NEED FOOD.

This is exactly what I needed to see.

Soft and sharp, like the wings of a butterfly, reads one caption on a photo of a girl showing off the remarkable angles of her stick-thin naked body, covering her nipples and vagina with spindly, oversized hands protruding from bony arms.

The headaches are a reminder of all we've lost, reads another caption accompanying a picture of a girl's thumb and forefinger encircling her wrist without touching it.

The space between my thighs is the valley of death I've traversed.

My body feels cold, but my mind and soul are blazing. The strength of beauty will triumph over the weakness of the body.

I hate the sound of my footsteps. They indicate my presence in the world. I want to be a thing without mass, devoid of matter, drained of all substance. I want to become nothing.

Such poetry. Such beauty.

As I scroll through the images, my free hand moves down the front of my panties, which I realize have grown damp. My eyes feast upon the photographs of delicate thighs beneath plaid miniskirts, the glorious ridges of jutting ribcages and protruding vertebrae, the sunken stomachs and ghostly faces. Looking at them fills me with the closest thing I've ever felt to love. It starts in my abdomen and blossoms like a stoked flame, spreading throughout my tremor-wracked body until the pleasure becomes so immense I have to cry out. I notice I've begun to weep, but I don't feel sad. I don't feel anything. There is nothing to do but lie there and let the tears come. They blur my perception of the angels on my screen and warp them into something nightmarish. Hollow demons with vacant black eyes and mouths full of static. I have to turn off my phone screen.

In the dark solitude of my bedroom, ragged with post-climax exhaustion, I can feel a little less alone knowing the angels are out there. That they're with me. That I'm one of them.

CHAPTER 12 – DISNEYLAND AFTER HOURS

One of the many great things about fasting is the euphoria you get somewhere around the twenty-two-hour mark. It sometimes comes sooner, other times later, depending on the size of your last meal and how much you've been eating lately in general. You'll develop a tolerance to it as you would with any good high, but as I've basically been gorging myself recently, my tolerance has eroded. When I'm first hit with the high the afternoon following Jasper's rejection, it's what I'd imagine Disneyland must be like for kids who are into that sort of thing. It's magic. It's better than coke, better than opiates. Certainly better than an orgasm. If I could feel like this all the time, I'd be unstoppable.

Roxette's "The Look" is playing on repeat as I dance naked around my apartment, stopping periodically in front of mirrors to admire my reflection, running my hands over my body, twisting to the rhythm, lip-syncing the words to the song. The slug is nowhere to be seen, and neither is the corpse girl.

I go shopping at the Beverly Center—which is oddly empty—and then at the similarly deserted Westgate in Century City. When I get home, I buy fifteen pairs of sunglasses from various luxury fashion sites. That night, I go to a shoot at a mansion in Sherman Oaks where I'm the prettiest girl there by miles. The theme is "Prom Night," except all the dresses are made out of frozen poultry meat and the male models are dressed as gigantic birds. I didn't go to my prom.

I don't eat anything for four days. The manic bliss comes and goes, sometimes leaving desolate dopamine crashes in its wake that cause me to break down into sobbing fits, hiding beneath my bed from something unseen that I imagine, for brief spells, is following me. These episodes tend to be short-lived and are only a minor inconvenience. Generally, I feel great. I feel better than ever.

After roughly 115 hours of being calorie-free, I wake around three AM shivering and drenched in sweat on my kitchen floor, about to stuff a handful of cashews into my mouth. Disgusted, I throw the bag of cashews in the garbage—I don't want to break my fast until day seven— and start toward my bedroom. A gurgling sound from the bathroom stops me mid-stride. The scent of rubbing alcohol and bleach comes from nowhere, saturating the air around me. There's another sound, too—a low, percussive thrumming. It's a sound like a disease.

A flip of the bathroom light switch reveals the fat girl in the mirror. The slug. Cheeks ballooned, eyes buried within bloated, pink mounds of flesh passing itself off as a face. Arms and thighs like slabs of meat. The bumps on her forehead have gotten bigger, and her mucus-coated skin has taken on a dark yellow-green hue. Slime is secreting from the mirror and sliding onto the sink.

"You're trying to kill me," she says. Her voice is guttural and raspy. "You can't kill me. You can try and try, but you'll never be rid of me."

"I already killed you. I'm already rid of you."

"If I'm dead, then who are you talking to?"

"I'm not talking to anyone." I shut off the light and run to my bedroom, diving into the bed and burrowing beneath the covers, pulling the sheets over my head. I lay still on my side for a long time, listening to my labored breathing, my irregular heartbeat. The sour, fruity smell of my breath collects beneath the blankets and smothers the lingering scent of cleaning supplies. Inhaling my own carbon dioxide becomes a consolation.

My consciousness is edging toward sleep when I sense a presence in the bed with me. A shifting. A rustling. Something cold moves across my bare abdomen. I open my eyes and look down. A narrow shape is laid across my stomach. When my vision adjusts to the darkness beneath the blankets, I realize it's an emaciated arm. The spidery hand is pressed flat between my breasts. It feels sticky.

Sitting upright, I pull the blankets back and flick on the lamp on my nightstand. There's no one in my bed, but there's a dark outline of what appears to be dirt and dead skin caked to the sheets.

"I'm not like she is," whispers a voice from behind me. I turn around to see the corpse girl standing in my bedroom doorway. The fingernails on her right hand are dripping blood onto the carpet. "I'm not a monster."

"How did you get out of the mirror?" I ask her, feeling hot tears on my face. "You're supposed to stay in the mirror."

"I was never in the mirror," she says.

* * *

I wake up beneath my bed the next morning, lying flat on my stomach. My first assumption is that last night's encounter with the corpse girl must have been a dream, but when I pull myself out from under the bed, there's a dark spot of maroon on the carpet where her fingers had been dripping blood. A smudged, crimson handprint is painted on my chest. The black outline is still present on the sheets, and there are black footprints all throughout the apartment. It seems there isn't anything to do but call my cleaning lady and tell her I need an emergency appointment.

CHAPTER 13 – KEROSENE LAMPS

Hal spends the first twenty minutes of our session crying because his set was apparently "a disaster" and none of his "so-called friends" he invited showed up. Even as he sobs, he doesn't take his sunglasses off. The lenses get fogged up as the tears collect behind them and spill over the sides. He keeps blowing his nose into a Versace handkerchief and calling me "cruel, just so fucking cruel" because I didn't come and support him. I make a lame, halfhearted attempt to excuse my absence, muttering a lie about a night shoot followed by a party I couldn't get out of, but he doesn't buy it. "It's just so *typical* of you," he whines. "You only ever think about yourself."

When he regains some semblance of composure after doing a couple bumps of coke, I ask if we can talk about me now. I cite the rate I'm paying him. "Sure, yeah, whatever," he says, sniffling. "I mean, fuck, if it's just about the *money* for you, then go off, I guess."

Already exhausted, not really following him, I say, "If...what's about the money? What else would it be about?"

He sniffles again. Wipes his nose with the hand-kerchief. "*This*," he says, spreading his arms, gesturing around the office. "You coming here, talking to me. I guess I thought we had a more complex relationship than something transactional. I thought we were supposed to *both* be there for *each other*."

"But you're...my therapist? And I don't think that's how it's...supposed to work?"

"Oh, *really*. Interesting. Tell me how it's *supposed* to *work*." He uses his fingers to draw air quotes around "supposed" and "work."

Shifting on the couch, adjusting my Dolce & Gabbana sunglasses, I say, "I pay you to...listen to me? And you're supposed to...I don't know, fix me?"

"Babe. No one can fix anyone. Besides, you don't even *need* fixing. I keep telling you, you're hot. You're a bombshell. You've got literally nothing to worry about, so I don't know why you're always so fucked up about everything. One of these days you'll listen to me and just...fucking...*chill*. And then you'll feel better."

"I don't actually think this is working out."

"Oh, please. Honey." He puts a hand to his chest. "Don't be so dramatic. This is normal. This is healthy."

"I'm starting to think that maybe it's not."

"What are you even going to do, huh?" His face darkens. His voice becomes edged with hostility. "Find another therapist? Start over from scratch? I mean, get real. You've been seeing me for *how* long? I *know* you. We have *rapport*. I know you better than *anyone*. The problem here is that *you* don't know *me*. I think these sessions would be a lot more productive if you took the time to listen to *me* for once."

"I really don't think that's...what the problem is. I don't think you ever listen to me. I'm lost and afraid and I don't know what to do." I can feel the tears coming, and this helpless knowledge fills me with an impotent rage. "The things that used to work aren't working anymore. I'm falling to pieces and no one cares and I...I just..." The next words get caught in a sob lodged in my throat. I lower my head and raise my hand to my face, covering my mouth and nose.

"Oh, Christ, don't tell me you're going to cry *again*. That's two sessions in a row."

"You cried first," I scream at him, feeling absurd and ashamed.

"Irrelevant. Absolutely irrelevant. Listen, let's just try

this, okay? Why don't I tell you about my childhood? Yeah? Does that sound good? Okay. So, I was born in Oklahoma, believe it or not. Never really fit in there, though. And when I was eleven, I—no, wait, was I twelve? No. I was eleven. Definitely eleven. When I was eleven, I..."

He drones on for the rest of the session, and I sort of tune him out, swallowing sobs and crying silent tears that mist up my sunglasses. He actually hugs me before I leave, and I'm too tired to do anything about it. He tells me this was "super productive" and that he thinks we've "made a hella crucial step in starting to figure things out."

In the Lyft home, the driver anxiously asks me if I'm okay. He's peering at me in the rearview mirror over the lenses of his sunglasses—I can't tell what brand they are, and I realize with a wave of sinking horror that he probably bought them off a rack at a gas station.

"Are you okay, miss?" he asks again. His face is contorted in obvious discomfort. He doesn't actually care if I'm okay. He just doesn't want to deal with a crying girl.

Shivering, I tell him to please turn the heat up.

CHAPTER 14 – DIET PASSION

My resolve to play it cool with Jasper finally shatters late one night when I take too much Xanax and decide it would be a good idea to take a Lyft to his apartment in Silver Lake. The driver is playing Christmas music the whole way there. I sit in the back seat looking out the window at the Christmas lights wrapped around the trunks of the palm trees, and I try to think back to a time when Christmas meant something to me. When it used to make me feel something. The memories are there somewhere, but I can't grasp them. They keep slipping through my fingers like water. Like mucus.

The front desk guy at Jasper's building calls Jasper to tell him he has a visitor, asking if he should send me up. He listens for a moment, and then lowers the phone, putting his hand over the receiver. He asks my name. When I tell him, he picks the phone back up and repeats it. He listens again for what seems like a long time, looking bored, glancing over at me with disinterest. The cold panic is a swarm of locusts in the back of my head. Furious tears bloom in my eyes, fogging up the lenses of my Chanel sunglasses. I blink them back, swallowing lumps in my throat. Finally, the front desk guy hangs up the phone and tells me I can go up.

Jasper comes to his door wearing a Tom Ford bathrobe and Matsuda sunglasses, a cigarette in his mouth and a crystal tumbler of whiskey in his hand. "Helen," he says, his voice toneless. "It's late. You should have texted."

"I'm sorry," is all I can say. "Is there...do you have

someone here?"

He takes the cigarette out of his mouth and stares at me blank-faced for a long time before saying, "No. There's no one here."

"Can I come in?"

Again, that hollow stare accompanied by a long, awkward silence, until he at last opens the door wider and steps aside to allow me to enter. It's been months since I've been inside his apartment, and the familiarity of its austere minimalism is at once a comfort.

"Do you want a drink?" Jasper asks as I take a seat on the red leather couch.

"Do you have White Claw?"

He stands there looking at me for a few seconds, holding his cigarette at an elegant angle that isn't quite feminine, but almost. "No," he says flatly. "I do not have White Claw."

"Nothing for me, then. Thanks."

He sits in the armchair across from me and takes a contemplative drag from his cigarette. The dim, blue-tinted lighting shimmers like water in the lenses of his sunglasses. "I don't know why you came all the way over here so late at night," he says.

I look away, out his floor-to-ceiling window at the glinting gold lights in the dark hills. "I guess I didn't want to be alone," I say. My voice sounds small. Compressed.

"Everyone is alone all the time. It doesn't matter if you want it. You can't get away from it."

Looking back at him, I say, "We're not alone right now."

"Yes, we are."

Rising to my feet, trying to ignore the rush of lightheadedness, I go to him and take the cigarette from between his fingers, putting it to my lips and pulling from it. I take the tumbler from him, too, dropping the cigarette into the remaining splash of liquor within it. Setting the glass on the little table beside his armchair, I climb astride him, slipping my hand inside his robe. The taut skin of his

66

chest is hard and warm. When I kiss him, it's like kissing emptiness. There's no substance, no real texture. He doesn't taste like anything. Diet Passion. A zero-calorie kiss.

In the dim light of his bedroom, he undresses me with staid fingers. There's no anticipatory tremulousness, no breathy excitement; his respiration is calm and even. The lack of enthusiasm is oddly soothing. His attention gives me only the most nominal amount of validation, stopping well short of slaking my thirst for it, but even this is pleasant, in a way. I'm gratified by the lack of gratification.

Laying me on the bed, he runs his palms over the hard contours of my body and says, "I love how fucking skinny you are." He keeps his sunglasses on when he enters me, and it's my image I see reflected in the lenses looming above me—not the slug's, not the corpse girl's...*mine*. Looking at the miniaturized versions of myself, I'm as beautiful as I've ever been. It's those twin reflections I focus on—not Jasper's hand in my hair, not the pressure of his cock between my slickened thighs, not the high-thread-count sheets beneath my back—and because of this, I almost come. Not quite, but almost, and this withheld pleasure is its own kind of bliss.

"You know where the towels are," Jasper says, collapsing beside me and lighting a cigarette. I get out of the bed and get a hand towel from the closet in his bathroom, wiping off my stomach and chest, the hollow of my neck. It's still me in the mirror, but the corpse girl is behind me, head bowed, stringy hair hanging in her wasted face.

"You can let yourself out," Jasper says when I come back into the bedroom. He's scrolling on his phone, smoking languidly, not looking at me. "I'd walk you down, but. You know. I don't feel like getting dressed."

"Sure," I say. "Um. Text me."

He looks over at me, inscrutable behind his dark glasses. "Text you about...what? What do you want me to...say?"

I don't answer right away. The void inside me—my

void, his void, consuming each other, becoming one—coils and pulses, spitting white heat. Staring out the glass door to his balcony, I see only an ocean of blackness. Unbroken. Eternal. "Nothing," I finally say. "You don't have to say anything."

Later, smoking a cigarette naked on my own balcony, I look at the ground so far below and wonder what it would feel like to fall. I wonder if I already know.

CHAPTER 15 – AN EMPTY CITY FULL OF GHOSTS

I have a week off before my next shoot, and on the first day I decide to go shopping. I wander around Rodeo, moving in and out of the shops, not paying a lot of attention to how much money I'm spending. Christmas music is playing everywhere. It's a cold day, and the sidewalks are deserted. No cars pass. The non-people working in the shops are the only other living things I see. I don't mind them as much as other non-people because they're occupationally required to recognize and acknowledge my elevated status as soon as I walk in the door. This is what I love most about luxury stores. The roles are clearly defined. I'm sure the staff are seething with hateful jealousy of their patrons, but all they can do is grin their cold, blank smiles and accommodate us.

In the Lyft ride home, shivering in the back seat amid enormous shopping bags rustling with tissue paper, I text Jasper and try not to hate myself for it. I also text Colette and Summer and, for the hell of it, someone I've saved in my phone as "Angel Dust Guy 3." If there'd ever been an Angel Dust Guy 1 or 2, they aren't in my phone anymore. I think about this as I wait for someone to reply, looking out the window at the cold, empty streets while the car zips beneath traffic lights that never turn red.

There's something like four million people in the city of Los Angeles but I never know where they are. It seems so vacant most of the time. No one is ever around when I need them. I want to believe I *don't* need them, that I'm entirely self-sufficient, but there are times when the city becomes so soul-crushingly lonely that I want to scream so someone will hear me. Times like these make me yearn for the claustrophobic anxiety of the parties I never want to go to, or even for the company of the other models who'd all see me dead if they had their way. At least our goals point in the same vague direction.

Inside my apartment, I drop the bags near the door to be opened at some other time, giving myself something to look forward to, and then I take off my clothes and sit crying on the floor of the bathroom for a little while. I make myself throw up even though I haven't eaten anything today; all that comes out is water and stomach bile. The corpse girl is waiting for me in the mirror, weeping blackish blood. "You're imaginary," I scream at her. "You're not real." A rash of purplish bruises begin to bloom beneath the gray skin stretched across her body. I look down at my own body and see the same bruises there, but they look older. Darker, with yellowed edges. I don't know how I didn't notice them before. The corpse girl giggles. It's a sound like the flicking tail of a rattlesnake.

Turning away from the corpse girl, I run a scalding bath and lower myself into the water, breathing in the steam and letting the heat thaw the frigid cold in my bones. I cry some more and pinch fingerfuls of flesh on the scant sections of my body where it's most ample. I want to cut them off with scissors. I want to be nothing but bone. I want to disappear.

Once my skin has pruned and droplets of sweat are plinking from my face and the back of my neck into the bathwater, I get out and towel myself off. Wrapping myself in a Versace bathrobe, I walk out of my apartment and begin drifting through the halls, imagining myself a ghost. I knock on doors that no one answers. I ride the elevator to different floors, praying to something that isn't there that I'll run into someone. Anyone. Maybe they'll ask me if I'm okay, take me inside, make me a cup of tea. Maybe some terrible man will grab me and tie me up and brutally rape me before cutting my face off so he can nail it to his wall. Maybe a girl will appear, a girl who's exactly like me, and she'll see me for what I am and take me in her arms and tell me everything is going to be all right. Maybe I'll even believe her.

None of these things happen. I don't see anyone. It occurs to me I've never seen any of my neighbors, and that maybe I'm the only person who lives in the whole building. Maybe I'm surrounded by demons and phantoms and poltergeists. Things long dead, or things which never lived.

Back in my apartment, I check my phone for texts. There are none. I check Instagram and Facebook for messages—nothing. The unread emails in my Gmail inbox are nothing but spam. Feeling desperate, I call Jasper. His phone rings one and a half times and then goes to voicemail. Colette's phone rings three times before playing a message saying her mailbox is full. Summer's phone just keeps ringing, and so does Zelda's. A mechanical voice tells me Angel Dust Guy 3's number has been disconnected.

It's three in the afternoon. The evening and subsequent night extend before me like stairs to a hangman's gallows. I think of lengthening shadows, of darkness, and it's too much. My stomach twists with hunger, insisting I feed it, but the thought of putting food in my mouth seems apocalyptic. Instead, I swallow two Valium and an Ambien, and then I lie down on my couch and wait for an inner darkness to take me before the outer dark has the chance to arrive.

A percussive thrumming sound from far away lulls me into an uneasy sleep.

CHAPTER 16 – BEYOND THE PLEASURE PRINCIPLE

Christmas comes and goes, and I don't hear from anyone. My mom is in Barbados on a trip she somehow won through her book club and doesn't have cell reception. I send texts that go unanswered and make fruitless phone calls that ring and ring until the droning tone becomes a sort of hypnotic solace. Increasing my drug intake allows the days to slide by in a muddled haze. It's in this haze that I attend my appointment with Hal, feeling strung out and exhausted, my eyes raw and bloodshot behind my Valentino sunglasses.

"Something about you occurred to me recently," Hal is saying. "It's something we need to, ah, rectify."

"What's that?" My voice sounds bubbly. Submerged.

"I don't know anything about you from a sexual perspective. We spend all this time talking about your hang-ups with food and being thin, and it's just getting kind of old. We need to explore new ground. We need to get sexual with it."

"I don't see how that's...relevant. I don't see what that has to do with anything."

"Oh, I'm sorry, *who's* the therapist here? Is it you? My sincerest apologies. I thought you paid *me* to know what's relevant to *your* recovery. But, yeah, if you've got this shit all figured out, let's keep talking about how sad you are, but also how happy being thin makes you, while *also* making you sad because you're happy. Yeah. Good plan. That's definitely working for you thus far."

I want a cigarette. "What do you want to know," I say, sighing.

Leaning forward, he says, "Let's talk about your first sexual experience. How old were you? What were you wearing? Was he older, younger? *Was* it a he? Or was it one of your girlhood friends? Maybe you were playing doctor, things got a little out of hand, so to speak, and then—"

"Jesus. Hal. Literally what the fuck."

"Okay, *fine*. Maybe you're not ready for that. No big. We can cover it in a later session. Why don't you tell me, then, what you like? What gets you off? How do you like to be touched? *Where* do you like to be touched? Are you into roleplaying? What's your preferred position? Do you enjoy the taste of semen? Do you like to—"

"Hal," I say, holding up my hand. "Stop. I'm really not getting what the point of this is. I don't feel comfortable talking to you about...those things."

He crosses his legs and drums his fingers on the armrest of his huge swivel chair. "Wow. Babe. I'm not gonna pretend like that doesn't sting a bit. You know me. And I'm *trying* to *help* you. I'm *trying* to peel back the *layers* of the *onion* that is *you*."

"I...get that. I just...don't feel like this is helping."

"Well, I'm not surprised, seeing as how you're not actually *doing* it. You have to commit. You have to put forth some effort. Look, I'm not super into Freudian philosophies, but I *do* think that everything is connected to sex in one way or another. We have to really get under the covers if we want to get to the heart of a matter."

I think of Jasper, whom I haven't heard from since my impromptu late-night visit. I wonder for a moment—only a moment—what Hal would say about that particular relationship, and then I realize I don't care. Getting to my feet, steadying myself with a hand on the wall to brace against the dizziness, I say, "I think I've had enough for one day."

Nonplussed, Hal says, "But our session isn't over."

74

"Yes, it is. I don't know why I keep coming here. You're not helping me. No one is helping me, but least of all you."

"You said something similar last time, but you came back to me."

"I need something you're not giving me. I need... direction."

"Babe, I can't give you that unless you meet me somewhere in the middle."

"I have to go."

"Where? Where do you have to go?"

"Away from here. Anywhere else."

As I'm leaving, he follows me into the hallway and shouts, "You'll be back. You always come back." And all I can do is hope he's wrong.

CHAPTER 17 – CANDLE WAX AND POLAROIDS

I somehow wind up at a New Year's Eve party at an art gallery in Silver Lake. I'm supposed to meet Colette here, but she texts me at the last minute to tell me she isn't going to make it. Something about a guy named Enclave and another party at a nightclub in Venice—or maybe Enclave is the name of the club; I don't know, I don't bother reading the whole text.

I'm standing outside smoking a cigarette when a guy my age stops on his way to the door. He takes off his Salvatore Ferragamo sunglasses and stares at me. He has the tall leanness and tanned, pretty-boy face of a model, which is probably what he is. Expensive haircut, Armani jacket and black T-shirt paired with Saint Laurent sweatpants and Balenciaga sneakers. Lots of gaudy rings and a heavy chain around his neck. The scent of too much cologne—Versace Eros, I think—wafts from him in waves. His eyes blaze with a coke-infused frenzy.

"Whoa, shit," he says, coming closer. "You look incredible. That dress. Who is it? Dior?"

"Celine," I say, adjusting my Hoorsenbuhs sunglasses and dragging from my cigarette. "It's from the fall collection."

"I adore it. Can I take a picture of you?"

I can't tell if he's hitting on me, or if he's just gay. It doesn't matter. I tell him sure and stare down the dark street with an exaggerated somberness, cocking my hip and holding my cigarette at an angle. He takes a digital camera from his pocket and drops to one knee. The light of the flash is baptismal. Here on the filthy sidewalk, surrounded by trash, I am washed clean.

"Who are you here with?" the guy asks. "I'm Dylan, by the way." He pronounces it *Dee-LAHN*, like it's French, but he doesn't have an accent. "Do you know Kenneth? Or Ryan? One of them owns this place but I can never remember which one." His words come fast, cramming into one another. He's worrying a wad of gum in his ever-clenching jaw.

"I don't know anyone," I tell him. "I was supposed to meet my friend here, but she blew me off to hang with some guy named Enclave."

Dylan tilts his head to the side. "Enclave. Like the club?"

"Um, yeah. Yeah. Like the club. Anyway, um, I'm Helen." I flick my cigarette into the street, watching the embers explode in the darkness.

"Helen. That's fantastic. Come inside, tell me more." He takes my wrist and leads me up the stairs to the gallery entrance. The bouncer glances at our wristbands, which came with the invitations, and steps aside to let us in.

For a gallery, there isn't much art. There are several bars and a number of lounge areas, and a main room with a wide dance floor and a stage upon which a laconic jazz band is playing. Clusters of people dance listlessly or stand around sipping their drinks and sucking on weed pens. Dylan's hand around my wrist keeps tightening and loosening with the rhythm of a heartbeat.

After ordering drinks—I stick with sparkling water—Dylan starts introducing me to people. He seems to know everyone. Their faces brighten at his approach, and they throw themselves upon him in lavish embraces. I pay close attention to people's body sizes, mentally calculating their BMIs. From what I've seen, I think I'm the thinnest girl here. The relief at this realization is almost enough to bring on tears, but I hold them back because I don't want to ruin my makeup.

I stick with Dylan because there isn't anything else to do. We flit around the gallery, and he has shouted conversations with pretty girls and boys over the din of the music while I mostly stand around taking drags from other people's vapes. Everyone keeps asking me if I'm having a good time. I tell all of them that I'm always having a good time. Nobody seems to detect the irony in my hollow smile.

Dylan pulls me into the men's room, and we do a few bumps in the stall. I'd been expecting him to make some kind of move, pressed up against each other like that, but he doesn't. Maybe it's the acrid scent of urine and vomit hanging in the air, but I don't detect any sexual energy from him at all. I wonder again if he's gay, though many of the women he's interacted with tonight have behaved with the suggestive flirtatiousness of past lovers, so I don't think that's it.

After leaving the stall, I stop in front of the mirror and take off my sunglasses, staring hollowly at my reflection. Am I bloated? Does my face look rounder than it did earlier tonight? Is my body retaining the two glasses of sparkling water I've consumed? I try to remember if I've urinated since arriving. I don't think I have. The cold panic sets in, coiling within my stomach. I don't have any particular interest in fucking Dylan, but why doesn't he want to fuck me? You can be anything as long as you're fuckable.

I blink, and the image of me in the glass is replaced by the slug. The bumps on her forehead have burst open, revealing antennae-like stalks. Her yellow-green skin is darker, edging into brown. She smiles, flashing sugar-eaten teeth shot through with black and yellow rot. "I keep trying to tell you," she says in a voice that sounds greasy. "You can't kill me. You *are* me."

"What are you looking at?" Dylan asks. He's standing in the doorway, waiting for me. Music comes in from outside the restroom. I search his face for something; I don't know what. The kinetic coke energy seems to vibrate beneath his skin.

I put my sunglasses back on and glance once more at my reflection. The slug is gone, but I still look somewhat bloated. "Me," I say. "I'm looking at me."

"Not a bad thing to look at," he says, pointing finger guns at me. It's a compliment, sure, but it isn't enough. It isn't nearly enough.

I can't keep living like this, I think. *I'm so exhausted.*

"I'll meet you out there," I tell Dylan. "Give me a second to powder my nose."

"*Powder your nose.*" He laughs. "Oh my God, I adore that. Do what you gotta do, babe."

When he's gone, I lock myself back in the stall and make myself throw up. Barely anything comes up. After I flush, the corpse girl looks up at me from the toilet water, her haunted face full of reproach.

I think I'm dying. I think I might actually be dying.

No one kisses me at midnight. I'd assumed Dylan would, but he opts for some girl in a sequined dress who looks like she's still in high school. The panic keeps twisting in my stomach, becoming a frenzied viper nest that makes me want to double over and shriek, but I keep it together.

While everyone is still cheering and blowing into noisemakers, some guy pulls his girlfriend onstage. One of the jazz players hands him a microphone. Everyone gets quiet after a moment, and the guy gives some saccharine speech to the girl before getting on his knees—both knees, not just one—and procuring a ring. She says yes, and everyone starts cheering again, and the jazz players begin playing a jubilant tune while pyrotechnics shoot from the back of the stage, and even with the coke I can't feel anything.

There seems no point in sticking around after that. I leave without saying goodbye to Dylan or any of the people he's introduced me to over the course of the night. I can't remember their names, anyway. The coat check guy gets me my coat and asks, "Leaving already?" When I say, "What do you mean, *already*?" he doesn't answer.

Instead of getting a Lyft right away, I walk down Sunset for a while, smoking cigarettes and shivering in the cold air. I think about calling Jasper because he lives somewhere around here, but to say what? What do you say to someone like that after midnight on New Year's Eve? I can't imagine he's alone, and even if he was, what difference would it make? We'd wake up tomorrow, and the date would be different, but everything else would be the same.

From the corners of my eyes, I keep thinking I'm seeing figures watching me. Dark shapes crouched near trashcans or peering from behind the palm trees. There's nothing there when I look, but I have trouble believing I'd imagined them, so I call a Lyft and wait on a bench, musing over the surprising emptiness of the boulevard. No cars, no pedestrians. Only ghosts.

CHAPTER 18 – PLEASURES IMPERMANENT

As I'm getting home from a shoot, the front desk guy stops me in the lobby and tells me I have a delivery. He disappears into the office and comes back pushing a dolly stacked with packages. In the elevator, riding up to the fifteenth floor, I can feel him staring at me. I adjust my Cartier sunglasses and act oblivious, uncaring, but inside there's a distinct sensation of regal triumph. *That's right*, I want to tell him. *Look at me. Lust for me. You are nothing, and I am everything. I am the embodiment of all you cannot have. You are fat and ugly and poor. Your kind exists only to serve my kind, and this is right and good.*

Inside my apartment, I tear into the packages, gently laying my purchases out on my bed. Seeing them gleaming and sparkling before me in the sunlight coming in through the floor-to-ceiling window, I'm overcome with a warm flood of emotion that feels very close to serenity. I have a contented peace and happiness that surges into the void inside me and spills over the brim. I'm drunk on it. The euphoria is of an almost chemical nature as I decorate myself with the dresses and shoes and sunglasses, posing in front of my mirror and snapping photographs. If I could feel like this all the time, I wouldn't need drugs. I wouldn't need anything.

It doesn't last. It never does. After the shiny new items have been put away in my room-sized closet, the rapture drains from me with the rapidity of a coke crash. The hollowness inside me is a moist cavern, bigger than even my wardrobe. I stand amid my countless outfits, my drawers of jewelry and various accessories, my racks of shoes, and I muse for the millionth time about how many I've never worn, probably will never wear. Sitting on the floor, I let myself cry for a while because there isn't anything else to do, and then I upload the pictures I took to Instagram. I keep refreshing my notifications, watching the likes and comments pour in, feeling tiny bursts of dopamine so short-lived they're almost insignificant.

I try to remember a time when my coping mechanisms worked sufficiently. When I could do things and they'd make me feel good without leaving me emptied and exhausted afterward. I believe such a time existed. I *know* it did, but I can't recall how it felt. Even before the perfect girl threw everything into disarray, my contentment with my life and my beauty and my thinness was always fleeting. This is a difficult truth to acknowledge, but if I'm honest with myself, it's impossible to deny.

I can't remember being happy for an extended period of time.

My life—for *years*—has been a series of exalting, godlike highs followed by devastating lows. The perfect girl was just another catalyst like so many before her.

But the slug, and the slime, and the corpse girl— they're new. The pattern of my discontent has become starker. My decline more precipitous.

MAKE YOURSELF FLAWLESS, the billboard told me.

Don't go so deep you can't make it back to the surface, Summer told me.

I can't even see the surface.

CHAPTER 18 – DREAMING OF HOW IT WAS SUPPOSED TO BE

My mom calls me to tell me she saw me in an issue of *Vogue* while standing in the checkout line at the grocery store.

"And Louanne," she's saying, "there was a time when I would have absolutely *gushed* to the person in front of me that *that's my daughter*, but honey, I just couldn't. All I could do was close the magazine and put it back. I didn't even *buy* it."

I'm sitting at my vanity, putting on makeup, getting ready to go to a party I don't want to go to. I look at the phone lying next to a container of blush, my mom's profile picture on the screen, the speakerphone icon lit up. I don't want to deal with her. I never want to deal with her. She's a relic from my past life. My dead life. Whatever purpose she once served has been outlived.

"Mother. If you have something to say, just say it."

"Sweetie, you're too *thin*. You don't *look* good. You look *sick*."

Two things happen inside me when people tell me this. The first is a recoiling, a guttural horror; I want to be perceived as perfect all the time, as the epitome of beauty, and to be told anything to the contrary is taken as a harsh blow to the face. The second is a rejoicing, a sick and gleeful satisfaction; being beautiful isn't enough...I have to be painfully, shockingly thin in order for it to work for me. I want to be so thin I disappear. If someone perceives this as an illness, it only means I'm succeeding. This is commitment. This is control. This is what it means to MAKE YOURSELF FLAWLESS.

These two reactions occur with dizzying simultaneousness. The potency of them both is such that they cancel themselves out. There's a moment of conflicted disorientation, but then it's gone, and I'm left with what I had before. Nothing changes.

"This life isn't *good* for you," she goes on. Her voice sounds strained. "It's not even what you *wanted*. You *wanted* to be a *filmmaker*. You were always so *talented* with a video camera."

"I can't keep having this conversation, Mom. I can't. We've been over this." Even as I say these words, I can't shake the feeling that the universe is trying to tell me something. That I'm reaching the point of no return. I think of the surface. Of how far away it is. Of how I don't know the way back to it.

"But *honey*, you've lost sight of what's *important*." She always sounds like she's whining, even when she's not. "Looks fade, you know."

"Only if you're poor."

"Louanne, *please*, you know I hate it when you *talk* like that. I didn't raise you to be classist."

"Ugly people and poor people are the same thing. That's not classism. It's capitalism."

"Capitalism *is* classist, honey." A pause on the other line. I can hear her breathing. Something about it sickens me. "*I* don't have a lot of money, you know. God knows I don't look like I used to. Do you think *I'm* ugly?"

"Mom. Please."

"I don't know what happened to you, Louanne." Her voice has suddenly deepened into a prickly coldness. "I really don't. It breaks my heart."

"I have to go, Mom." I realize there are tears in my eyes, which is annoying because it means I'll have to fix my makeup. I look away from the mirror for only a second in order to end the call, but when my eyes return to it, both the slug and the corpse girl are standing behind me.

86

"She doesn't know what she's talking about," says the corpse girl, running the jagged fingernails of her blood-stained right hand through my hair. It's a pleasant sensation. From somewhere far away, I can hear the thrumming heartbeat sound, stricken and ominous. "You're getting more beautiful every day."

"*No*," the slug booms in her greasy voice, the stalks on her forehead twitching. "Listen to your mother. *YOU NEED TO EAT.*"

"Leave me alone," I plead to both of them. "I'm begging you. Just let me have my old life back. The one where being thin and beautiful was enough. Where I was happy."

"It was never enough," says the corpse girl. "You were never happy."

And I want so badly for her to be wrong even though I know she isn't.

At the party, someone asks why there's ketchup in my hair.

CHAPTER 19 – NOTHING ELSE

"**M**y mom says I'm too thin. She says I've given up on my dreams."

Jasper peers at me over the lenses of his Moscot sunglasses. "There's no such thing as too thin," he says. "As for your dreams, I mean, Jesus. Dreams? Who has dreams? What does she think you are, eight?"

We're sitting in a booth at La Boheme on a Saturday afternoon about a week after the conversation with my mother. He's drinking a gin and tonic; I'm drinking a White Claw. The Xanax I took earlier has turned the volume down on everything. Made it all more palatable. "Don't you have dreams?" I ask. "You used to talk about writing a novel."

He snorts. Rattles the ice in his tumbler before taking a long sip. "A *novel*," he says, as though the word is distasteful. "Do you know how much money there is in *novels*? None. Fucking zilch. Look at me. Look at how I'm dressed. Look at the car I drive, the apartment I live in. People dream of my life. I am the dream."

"Right, yeah," I say, noncommittal. I look at my reflection in the dark lenses of his glasses and see the corpse girl. Mottled gray skin stretched across brittle bones, stringy hair caked with dirt. I shut my eyes behind the lenses of my Burberry sunglasses, blocking her out. "But don't you ever want to..." I trail off, not sure where I'm going with it. I try to find the thread, but I can't.

"Don't I ever want to what," he says. "Want? What is there to want but more of what I already have? I mean, what do you want? You have most of what I have. You're rich, you're thin, you're beautiful. What else is there?"

"I don't know. I don't know what else there is. I guess there isn't anything else."

We go back to his apartment and have empty sex that leaves me appropriately unfulfilled. Afterward, we go to a new club downtown called No Cap that some guy Jasper knows just opened last weekend. Pressed against him on the dance floor, moving passionlessly to the beat of a synthy pop remix of "Love Shack," I can pretend like everything is all right. The cold panic feels far away. Here amid this mass of sweating bodies, I can't smell the bleach and the rubbing alcohol. I don't see any mucus anywhere. The slug and the corpse girl aren't here right now.

But then a trio of girls who know Jasper invite us to come hang out in their VIP booth, and the night comes apart. I can tell that two of them have slept with him, and the third one is jealous of this fact. Jasper's attention is diverted and refocused upon them, and I become a forgotten piece of the scenery. This goes on for the better part of an hour, until one of them whispers something in Jasper's ear and he nods, his face serious and composed. Looking at me, he says over the music, "We're gonna split."

Blinking behind my sunglasses, I say, "Who's...we?"

"Me and um...them." He looks at the girls with an expression that approaches apology but doesn't quite get there. "I, uh, don't remember any of your names." He shrugs. They giggle and don't say anything.

"But what about...me?" I ask. I hate how it sounds but I can't not say it.

"What about you?" he asks back, looking bewildered.

I swallow several times in quick succession. "But you...drove me here?"

"So...get a Lyft? I mean, seriously, Helen. Come on. Don't be difficult."

When I get home, I make myself throw up even through there isn't anything inside me but bloody mucus.

The corpse girl holds my hair back.

CHAPTER 20 – CLOSER

"**I**'m starting to think Jasper isn't good for me," I'm telling Colette one night at a party on the rooftop of the Ace Hotel downtown. "I'm starting to think he's maybe a really bad guy."

"Jasper?" Colette sips her martini and looks out at the city through the glass partition at the building's edge. "I don't know. I don't think he's so bad. I once hooked up with this wannabe screenwriter who made me eat used Q-tips, so."

"Q-tips? That he'd...cleaned his ears with? Like, you actually...ate them?"

"Look, what I'm trying to tell you is it can always be worse."

"Yeah," I say, lighting a cigarette. "I guess." And then I whisper, "Everything is falling apart. I'm breaking down."

Colette must not hear me, because she says, "Bitch, did you hear about Gretchen?"

"Gretchen," I repeat. "No. Um. I don't know...um, I don't think I know a Gretchen."

Colette pushes her Prada sunglasses down the bridge of her nose so she can peer at me wide-eyed over the lenses. "Gretchen *Carter*, bitch. You know her. She runs that cute vintage shop in Santa Monica that her hedgie bro husband bought for her. *Anyway*. She had a *miscarriage*. Like, *one month* before she was *due*. She had to deliver the dead baby and everything."

"Oh. That's really...sad. I didn't know she was... pregnant." I still don't know who Gretchen is.

"Bitch, that's not even the worst of it. She's totally lost her shit. She keeps posting these weird TikToks of her crying while holding a headless baby doll. Here, I'll show you her latest one." She pulls her phone out of her Gucci purse and shows me a video of an overweight woman sitting cross-legged on a beach somewhere, staring into the camera, sobbing. The baby doll cradled in her arms is indeed headless. The noise of the party happening around us makes it hard to discern what music is playing in the video, but I think it's Enya.

"Whoa," I say, hitting my cigarette. "Was she always that fat?"

"No, bitch, you *know* her. She used to be hot. That's just leftover baby weight."

I shake my head. "People always think pregnancy is an excuse to gain weight and, like, it just...is not an excuse at all."

"I think that's maybe a *little* harsh," Colette says, putting her phone away. "But I basically get what you're saying." She finishes her drink and then pulls me through the crowd to the bathroom, where we do a few lines off the edge of the sink. Someone has scrawled "DIE WOKE SCUM" in purple lipstick on the mirror. I sort of disassociate a little as the corpse girl watches me from behind the glass, black tears seeping from her ghost eyes.

I lose Colette in the crowd shortly after we leave the bathroom, so I wander around the party, smoking cigarettes and sipping a White Claw. A lot of the vacant faces look familiar, but I don't feel like I know any of them. They all seem vaguely hostile.

I end up on a couch listening to a teenage boy in a Brooks Brothers suit and vintage Preciosa sunglasses shout over the music about the evils of cryptocurrency and its downstream effects on the environment. I want to tell him I don't care about cryptocurrency or the environment. I want to tell him how hard it is to care about anything. These are things I want to tell him, but it seems easier to tell him we should go back to my place.

In the darkness of my bedroom, I apologize for the smell of bleach and rubbing alcohol, explaining with a flippant lie that my cleaning lady was here earlier. He looks at me kind of funny but then shrugs and starts to get undressed. He leaves his sunglasses on.

"Tell me I'm beautiful," I keep saying to him while I'm on top of him. "Tell me I'm sexy. Tell me I'm skinny. Tell me I'm the skinniest girl you've ever seen." I give him these specific instructions over and over, but he won't do it. He doesn't say anything. He runs his hands over my body, staying very quiet, his face set in an absurd grimace of concentration. Like he's trying to focus on a test. I let him come on my face when it's over even though I don't want him to.

In the bathroom, the corpse girl crawls out of the mirror with the skittery movements of an insect and licks my face clean. Her tongue has wet, downy fur on it. She runs a long, bloodstained fingernail along my jawline and says, "You're getting closer."

"To what?" I ask, but she only smiles and crawls back into the mirror, facing away from me, her narrow shoulders hunched. I tell her to look at me, but she doesn't turn around. The thrumming sound is pulsing rhythmically from some unknown place, and the corpse girl sways to its sickly beat. "Sometimes I feel like you hate me," I say. "And other times I feel like you love me. I can't figure out which one it is. I can't figure out if it makes any difference."

The boy is gone when I return to the bedroom. I can't remember how long I was in the bathroom, but it doesn't matter. I decide I'm going to sleep under my bed again tonight. Lying flat on my back, staring up at the bottom of the mattress through the mesh of the bedframe, I almost feel safe.

CHAPTER 21 – LIGHTS IN CHAOS

"I think I need to...do something," I tell Jasper in bed one morning after going a whole week without texting him. "I think I'm really...falling apart."

He's on his phone, scrolling Instagram and smoking a cigarette with his oversized Tom Ford sunglasses on. He lowers the phone and swivels his head toward me. "Do something like...what? Like...hot yoga?"

"No, not like hot yoga. I can't stop...starving myself. And I'm afraid that I'm going to...I'm really starting to get scared, Jasper. I can't stop, and it keeps getting worse, and I think maybe I'm going to die." I take a breath, feeling the sting of tears behind my eyes and fighting them. "I think I need to go somewhere. Like, a treatment center."

"Oh." He looks back down at his phone, resumes scrolling. "Just don't get fat. If you get fat, we're done."

"No, yeah. I mean, of course. I won't get fat. I can't. I couldn't let myself get fat."

"You think that now. Look, I hope you're right. I hope you know what you're doing. But so many girls go to these...I don't know, these facilities, and then they just totally blow up. We're talking cow status. We're talking complete fucking land whales."

"I won't let it happen." I glance at my wall-mounted mirror on the other side of the room. The slug is there, grinning. Almost all of her human qualities have morphed into something gastropodous—her limbs have been absorbed into the slimy, gelatinous mass of her body, and the stalks on her forehead are nearly a foot tall. Mucus seeps from the edges of the glass, dripping down the wall into a wet spot on the carpet.

I tear my gaze away from the mirror to see Jasper staring at me. Twin images of the corpse girl look out from the huge lenses of his sunglasses. She's barely more than a skeleton. Most of her skin and hair are gone. Her eyes remain, vacant and fathomless, full of longing and regret. "What?" I say to Jasper, lowering my eyes so I don't have to look at the corpse girl.

He scratches his jaw. "I'm just looking at you. I mean, you don't look *that* thin. You're thin, but, like, the right amount. I don't think you're emaciated, or whatever. I think you might be overreacting. Have you tried, like...cutting back?"

"Cutting back on...what?"

"Um. The coke?"

"The...What does the coke have to do with anything?"

Cocking his head, he says, "Isn't that why you want to go to rehab? You're doing too much coke and you don't have an appetite?" Apparently detecting something in my face, he adds, "Sorry, I don't know. I must have missed something."

"It's not the coke, Jasper. It's not drug rehab." I take his cigarettes and light one, reaching over him to pick up the heart-shaped ashtray on the nightstand so I can set it between us on the bed. "Just forget it."

"I guess I don't know why you're telling me about whatever this is."

"I'm not. We're dropping it. It's fine, we don't have to talk about it."

"Do you need a ride to this place, or something? Because I can't promise I'll be available."

"No, Jasper. No, I don't need a ride."

"Cool. That's good. I'm, you know, really busy. And I have...a lot of things...going on. In my life."

"Yeah, no, of course. I know that."

"Good. I mean, you should. Know that. Anyway, just...remember what I said. Don't get fat. I won't even be able to look at you if you get fat."

The slug laughs from her place in the mirror.

After Jasper leaves, I call Hal. He answers by saying, "Well now. It's been a while. I knew you'd come crawling back. Although, I *will* admit, you've stayed away longer than I'd anticipated."

"I'm not calling for an appointment," I tell him. "I need you to send me a list of...I need some names of eating disorder clinics."

Silence on the other end of the line. It lasts a long time. When he speaks, he says, "Babe. You don't want to do that."

"I don't know if I want to yet or not. I'm still...weighing options. I haven't made up my mind. But I want some names of places in case that's the route I decide to go."

"Babe, I'm *begging* you. Don't go that route. Girls who go that route turn into—"

"Complete fucking land whales, yeah. I've been told." I swallow. "Listen. I didn't call to argue about this. I just want some names of places. That's all."

"He*len*," he whines, drawing my name out. "*Please.* I'm *telling* you, this is not something you want to do." I realize from the broken sound of his voice that he's started to cry.

"Like I said. I don't know if it's something I want to do. But I want to have the option. Look, I can always just Google places if I have to, but I don't want to do that. I shouldn't have to do that. This is *your* job. *Do* your *job.*"

"You haven't even been *paying* me," he wails.

"I've paid you literally thousands of dollars," I scream back at him. "You never did anything for me. Do this one thing."

"*Fine,*" he says, sounding like an obstinate child. "But just know that I don't agree with it." He sniffles. I listen to him blow his nose for a long time, and then he says, "I'll email you some places tonight." He blows his nose again. "They're going to be expensive, you know."

"I don't care. Just send them to me."

"I *said* I *would*, so I *will. God*, you haven't changed a bit."

"You have no idea."

"Will you come see me when you get out? Only if you stay thin, though. If you wind up getting fat, I don't want to see you. I have a strict rule against fat clients. I think that's technically illegal so I'll deny it if you tell anyone, but I feel like I can tell you things."

"Goodbye, Hal."

When I hang up the phone and lock the screen, the corpse girl is looking up at me from the black glass. "Don't do it," she says.

"I don't know what I'm going to do," I tell her.

CHAPTER 22 – TAKE IT ALL THE WAY DOWN

I come out of a Xanax blackout around three PM on a Saturday at the La Brea Tar Pits. The reasons for being here are mysterious but don't seem worth exploring. I'm standing in front of the Lake Pit—which is filled not with mucky water, as it should be, but with mucus that reeks of rubbing alcohol and bleach—staring at the statues of the mammoths. The one I imagine to be the mother mammoth is halfway submerged in the slime, its head angled upward, its trunk and tusks pointed at the sky. Its mouth is open in what can only be a scream. On the shore is a baby mammoth and another adult mammoth, which I decide is the father. The baby is also screaming. Its trunk is reaching helplessly toward its struggling mother. The father doesn't seem to give a shit.

Feeling tears on my face, I turn away from the statues and briefly take my Tiffany sunglasses off to wipe my eyes with the back of my hand. I'd normally feel embarrassed to be crying in public, but there isn't anyone around. I've been here a few times for photoshoots, and it was always crowded, but today the starkly sun-dappled grounds are completely deserted.

I wander westward, past the enclosed pits of chemically scented slime, past the Observation Pit, to a sea of white-brown gravel in front of a long, imposing building that doesn't appear to be in use. There's a rambling walkway cutting through the gravel, dipping beneath the ground's surface, with an enormous boulder affixed atop the walkway's midpoint. Standing beneath the boulder is a dark figure. It's too far away to make out its features, but I know with inexplicable certainty it's the corpse girl.

The sound of music—a Rolling Stones song, I think—cuts through the uneasy silence. Following it, I turn left and walk into a wide cement courtyard. There are empty picnic tables everywhere and closed-up food trucks lining the perimeter. The source of the music is revealed as some kind of street musician, plucking at a lute with unusually long fingers, standing alone on the far side of the courtyard. I approach him, feeling both magnetized and unnerved. He's tall and lean and dauntingly handsome, with alabaster skin and stylishly tousled dark hair, wearing stonewashed jeans and a burgundy leather jacket over a black T-shirt with bold yellow text which reads, "BRING JESUS INSIDE YOU." His feet are clad in snakeskin cowboy boots the same deathly white shade as his skin. He isn't wearing sunglasses, and his irises are a hue so black and deep they nearly become one with his pupils. There's a velvet black top hat before him, stuffed to the brim with three-dollar bills. As I draw nearer to him, he stops playing the lute and smiles. It's a terrible smile—too wide, too white, too many teeth. I want to run, and I almost do, but then he says, "Where are the ships?"

I blink behind my sunglasses, feeling cold and sick. "What?"

His wicked grin widens, and the horrible sight of it seems to produce, for a moment, a deafening static in my head that makes it feel as though it will crack open. But then the smile shrinks into something normal, something pleasant, and the static stops. "Helen Troy," he says. "With a face to launch a thousand ships. That's you, isn't it? Only...where are the ships? *Have* they yet launched for you? *Will* they *ever*? All your hard *work*, all your *suffer*ing, and for what? Who's coming to save you?" He looks around the empty courtyard in mock wonder. "I don't see anyone. I don't think anyone's coming."

Feeling colder, feeling sicker, I say, "Who are—Have we worked together? Have you done any...modeling?"

The amiable smile turns into a frown in such an instantaneous flash it's like he'd never been smiling at all. "Heavens *above*," he says, shaking his head. "I will never under*stand* the ab*surd* questions people ask me." His black eyes blaze. "No, Helen. No, *Louanne*. We have not *worked* together. I have *not* done any *mod*eling."

His utterance of my old name, my dead name, conjures an overwhelming nausea in my stomach. If I'd eaten anything today, I'd surely throw it up. "Then...then how do you...how do you know my name? How do you know...both of my names?"

The smile returns—awful at first, stretching across his whole face, before normalizing back into the pleasantly human grin. "I know *every*thing, sweetheart." Then, holding up a freakishly long index finger, he amends, "Well, except calculus."

"This is a dream," I say distantly. "I'm imagining this. You aren't real."

"Well, *that's* not very *nice*." He shakes his head, clucking his tongue. "You people. You're always telling yourselves I'm 'not real.' That I'm *imagin*ary. And yet..." He gestures at his lanky body and spreads his arms out, cocking his head and winking at me. "Here I am." Pointing his creepy finger at me, he says, "*You*, though. *You're* becoming less real by the *minute*. Wasting away into nothing. Before long, there won't be anything left."

"Don't skinny shame me."

He laughs. A sound like old, dead music on a broken record player. "*Shame* is the *name* of the *game*, summer child. You don't need *me* to give it to you, either. You've got *plen*ty of it all on your own."

"What am I supposed to do?" I ask before I can stop myself. "I don't know what to do."

"Don't you, though? Haven't you *always* known? You've made the decision already. You keep making it over and over again. You just can't com*mit* to it. And, as I said, *no one* is coming. You are *alone*. There's no armada of ships on their way to save you. What*ever* you do, you have to do it by your*self.*"

"You're speaking in riddles."

"Am I speaking in riddles, or are you just not bright enough to keep up? Starvation *does* impair one's cognitive ab*ilities*, you know."

"What do you want from me? What are you trying to tell me?"

The look he gives me is full of condescending pity. "I don't want anything from you. I couldn't give fewer good golly goshdamns *what* you do. Eat, don't eat. It makes no difference to me. But...*look*, I can *see* you're really struggling here. So, the question you have to ask yourself is this—what is beauty worth? Really, truly ask yourself that, and then really, truly answer it."

"I already have. It's worth everything."

He narrows his eyes and purses his lips in an expression of dubiousness. "Is it, though? I mean, to *you*—is it? On a *purely* sub*ject*ive basis as it pertains to you, and you speci*fically*, is it *honestly* worth everything? Do you know what that *means*, and what will happen if the answer is yes?"

I don't answer. Instead, I look in the direction from which I'd come. I can't see the corpse girl—she hasn't followed me—but I know she's there, lurking around somewhere. Waiting.

"No one is coming," the street musician says again. "But something *is* waiting."

Returning my gaze to him, I say, "Do you want to come home with me?"

He smacks me upside the head. Not hard enough to hurt, but hard enough to jostle my sunglasses loose. I straighten them as he says, "Girl. For *real*. *Get* your *shit* to*gether*." Giving me a curt head shake of consternation, he lifts his lute and resumes playing the Rolling Stones tune, his freaky fingers moving in an effortless blur across the strings.

There's nothing else for me to do but leave.

I text Jasper from the back seat of the Lyft on the way home, but there's no reply.

CHAPTER 23 – MY NAME IS HELEN TROY

The day after my encounter with the spooky street musician, I spend the morning tearfully trying to throw up because I feel like there's food inside me even though I know there isn't. It's after a few hours of gagging over the toilet that I make my decision. I have to do something. I can't keep living like this. This is not living. I'm exhausted. I'm so exhausted.

As I kneel shivering in front of the toilet, there's a distinct sensation that I have a narrow window in which something can still be done. In which I can maybe save myself from the encroaching hell. This sensation is coupled with the knowledge that if I don't seize upon the window, it will close forever.

The first thing I do is call my agent and tell him I'm going to be taking some time off. Yes, everything is okay. No, I don't know when I'll be back. *Et cetera.*

I then pack a Louis Vuitton suitcase with a week's worth of clothes, along with nine of my favorite pairs of sunglasses. The clinic I select from the list Hal emailed me is a place in Malibu called Along the Path Forward. I choose this particular one because it's the first one on the list, and because I like how the name sounds. For a moment, I think about calling them, but I decide against it. I'm afraid if I call them, I'll get cold feet. Better to just show up, where it'll be harder to back out.

The slug is conspicuously absent as I get ready to leave, and I can't help but find this unnerving. She should be here, gloating. Taunting me. Reveling in her presumed victory. The fact that she isn't here seems off. It makes me think something is wrong. Something is out of sync.

The corpse girl follows me around the apartment, not saying anything. I thought she'd be crying, pleading with me not to go, but she remains silent, and the only sound is the percussive thrumming noise coming from somewhere unseen. She's in the back seat of the Lyft with me as we head to Malibu, her dead face devoid of expression. Staring at me.

The driver doesn't seem to notice.

* * *

There's soft meditation music playing in the lobby. Like what you'd hear at a spa. The girl at the front desk is my age, and she could be mildly pretty if she lost maybe twenty pounds. She's talking to a tall, tan guy in his fifties in a long white coat. Their eyes move to me as I approach the desk, and something shifts in their faces. It's strange—there's something like trepidation in their eyes, as though they expect me to be dangerous.

As I get closer, the guy—the name badge on his coat identifies him as Dr. Charles Keyes—folds his arms over his chest and regards me with a stern face. The girl smacks her gum and leans back in her chair, rapidly clicking her ballpoint pen.

"Yes, um, hello," I say, adjusting my Linda Farrow sunglasses and fidgeting with my hands. "I need to, um...I need to—"

"You can't be here," Dr. Keyes says.

"Should I call security?" the girl asks him, eyeing me cruelly.

"No, no, I don't think that's necessary," Keyes tells her. Sighing, he runs his hand through his sandy blond hair that's gone white at the temples. "She's not going to make any trouble." He takes off his glasses and folds them into the pocket of his coat. "Are you?" he asks me.

"I...no, I'm not going to—um, I'm sorry, but...what? I don't know what you're talking about."

"You need to leave," he says. "We've been over this."

"I'm sorry," I say again, feeling lightheaded. "But I...I think you have me mistaken for someone else."

And then he says, "Louanne. Or, I'm sorry, *Helen*. There's nothing more we can do for you. Not here. As I've said, you need a very specific kind of psychiatric treatment that we're not equipped to provide."

"I...I don't understand. I've...I've never even been here before."

Keyes and the girl exchange a glance.

"Is this some kind of sick joke?" I ask. "Who put you up to this?"

"Are you hearing voices again?" Keyes asks. "Seeing things? The slug? The dead girl? The mucus? Smelling the phantom scent of...what was it? Cleaning agents, right?"

My vision narrows into a thin vertical strip. My pulse reverberates in my ears. A chill washes through my veins, and I sway on my feet.

"Oh, Jesus, I think she's gonna faint," I hear the girl say from far away.

"Goddamn it. Get up, give her your chair."

Movement in the limited field of my vision. Firm hands on my shoulders. A falling sensation as I'm lowered into a sitting position. A garbled voice telling me to "breathe, just breathe, slow breaths in and out."

When my vision clears and the world comes back into focus, Keyes and the girl are standing over me. They don't look too concerned. More annoyed than anything.

"When was I here before?" I ask. My mouth is dry. My palms are slick with sweat.

"Do you truly not know?" Keyes asks, his voice gruff and impatient.

"I...no, I...I guess I don't. I don't remember ever being here."

"For fuck's sake," says the girl. She turns on her heel and stalks away, shaking her head and muttering.

"What the hell is her problem?" I ask.

"Marlene Lennox is a close friend of hers," Keyes says, as if that's supposed to mean something.

"Who is Marlene Lennox. I don't know who that is."

"She used to be a nurse here. You attacked her during your last stay. You were detoxing from an extremely high quantity of narcotics, and you clawed her face with your nails. Quite viciously, actually. Reconstructive surgery was attempted. It was not entirely successful."

"That's not possible. I wouldn't do something like that. And if I did, I would remember it."

"Like you remember the three separate occasions you've checked yourself in here, only to leave against medical advice every time?"

"Three," I breathe, the lightheadedness swimming back. I think suddenly of the street musician with the horrible grin. *You've made the decision already*, he'd said. *You keep making it over and over again.* "That's...that's not...you're saying I've been here more than once?"

"That is what one could deduce from *three separate occasions*, yes."

"How long did I stay for?"

"You were here for almost a week the second time. The first and third times were only for a few days. I have no reason to believe this time would be any different, which is why I must again ask you to leave. Honestly, I'd 5150 you to a state facility if California still allowed us to do that kind of thing. You're a danger to yourself and others, and you need serious, long-term treatment. This is an eating disorder clinic, not a goddamn nut ward. If you're serious about getting help this time—I don't believe you are, but *if* you are—I'd urge to you to go straight to the nearest hospital and let them figure out what to do with you."

Rising cautiously to my feet, I say, "Um, okay. Yeah. Yeah, I'll...I'll do that."

The look he gives me could draw blood. "See, I don't think you will. Because at the end of the day, you don't care about anyone but yourself. But your self-interest is so delusional and misguided that you don't even know what's actually good for you."

"That's not fair. You don't know anything about me."

"On the contrary, I know much more about you than I'd care to know. Goodbye, Louanne. Or Helen, or whatever it is you're calling yourself these days."

I look around at the white walls, the gleaming floors, the arched ceiling. The motivational posters, the rack of antidepressant brochures. I look at the old man in front of me. At the vacant front desk. I look at it all and I wonder to myself, *What am I doing here?*

Something comes over me. A resolve. A blinding clarity.

Along the Path Forward, this place is called.

I know my path forward. I've always known.

"It's Helen," I say. "My name is Helen Troy."

Saying those words has an instant palliative effect. It's a reassurance, a comfort. I *am* Helen Troy. I'm *not* Louanne. I'll never be Louanne again.

"I'm leaving," I say, more to myself than to Keyes. "I won't be back."

"Best of luck to you," he says with a tight smile. "I hope I never see you again."

Outside, I open the Lyft app while shivering beneath the cold sun, smoking a cigarette. *Where are you going?* the text on the screen asks me. There isn't any hesitation as I key in my home address. When the car arrives, I huddle into the back seat, pulling my knees to my chest and telling the driver to turn the heat up.

CHAPTER 24 – MAKE YOURSELF FLAWLESS

When I get back to my apartment, the corpse girl is waiting for me. She pulls me into an embrace that feels more like home than anywhere else ever has.

I momentarily consider calling my agent back to tell him I've reconsidered my sabbatical, but the corpse girl talks me out of this. She tells me I deserve some time off. I can lose some more weight. Relax. Shop. When I do decide to go back to modeling, I'll be rested and happy, and thinner and more beautiful than ever before. This sounds like a lovely idea.

Immediately, I cut out almost all calories. I fast for days at a time, and on the rare occasions when I eat, it's a strict diet of water, celery, lettuce, and the occasional apple. This regimen gives me renewed purpose. I feel like I'm accomplishing something. I watch the pounds keep sloughing off day after day. At night, I sleep with my scale hugged to my chest like a teddy bear. It tells me the most wonderful things. I love it almost as much as I love the new, improved me.

The mirror rewards my progress, too, especially after the first couple weeks. It shows me such exquisite sights. My bones have never been more pronounced. My skin glows. My hair is thick and luscious. My eyes shine with ethereal brightness.

Perhaps best of all, the slug is gone. There's no mucus anywhere. It's only me and the corpse girl now, but I've realized she *isn't* a corpse. That was my eyes playing tricks on me. She's an *angel*. She's the ideal me. She's flawless and beautiful in every way, and she loves me. She wants me to be as happy and beautiful as she is. I'm not there yet, but I'm getting there. I'm getting very close.

There is some pain, yes, and some weakness, but the drugs help with that. I don't know where they keep coming from, because I never leave my apartment, but there's a seemingly endless supply of them. Coke, uppers, down-ers—everything I could want. If I take enough of them, it quiets my earthly body's protests against the emergence of my heavenly self.

After I've been engaged in my new routine for roughly a month, I'm startled from a Valium-induced daze by a knock at my door. Shivering, I limp to the peephole and look out into the hallway, but my vision is too bleary to see who it is. It looks like a male, but I'm not certain even of that. When I call out for the visitor to identify himself, he answers, "It's Jasper. Um. The front desk guy let me come up? I guess he recognized me, and...I told him I was doing a...wellness check?"

"Jasper," I whisper. This name once meant something to me, and not even all that long ago. But now...now, there's no emotion connected to it at all. "You should have texted," I call out to him.

"I did. I've been texting. And calling. For, like, a week and a half. I hadn't heard from you, and..." He trails off. "Look, just let me in, will you?"

I suppose it's possible that he's texted and called; I haven't been checking my messages. The only thing I use my phone for these days is shopping.

When I open the door, the blurry image of Jasper is standing there wearing Garrett Leight sunglasses and an Armani suit. I think maybe he's gotten a haircut, but I can't be certain. He stares at me for a second and then raises his hand to his mouth. "Helen," he says. "What...my God."

"I know," I say, lifting my eyes and giving him a little shrug of mock modesty. "Here, come in." I step out of the way and open the door wider, leaning against it. Jasper keeps staring at me for another few moments before entering the apartment like he's in some kind of daze. "I'm aware that my new beauty might be a little jarring. I read somewhere that the angels in the Bible were so beautiful they were terrifying." I shut the door and smile at him.

Rubbing the back of his neck, Jasper says, "I don't think...I don't think that's totally true. I think they were just...terrifying." He looks me up and down, shifting uneasily on his feet. "I mean...Jesus, Helen." Glancing around my apartment, he adds, "Why are there...black footprints all over your carpet?"

Still grinning at him, I undo the sash on my Coco de Mer robe and shrug it from my shoulders, letting it fall into a silken pool around my ankles. Jasper makes a face and takes a step backward. I spread my arms, imagining they're wings. "Look at me," I say. "I'm so close to perfect. I'm making myself flawless."

"Fucking Christ, Helen. What have you done."

"I've self-actualized. I've evolved. I've become something so much better than I ever was before."

"You look gross. Like, literally disgusting." He runs his hand through his hair. "I mean, look. I know I've always said there's no such thing as too thin. But this...Helen, this is too thin. This is just...so gross."

My brain receives these words but doesn't process them. It turns them over and refashions them into something else.

"I feel so wonderful, Jasper. I don't need you anymore. I have *me*, and *me* is almost perfect. I'm getting closer every day."

"I don't...I don't understand. You were...I thought you were going to some treatment center. To, like...get help, or whatever."

"I don't know what you're talking about," I say, beaming down at my body, rubbing my hands over its comforting contours and notches. "Treatment for what? I don't need help with anything. I'm in total control."

"No, I...I don't think this is what control...looks like."

"I don't need you," I tell him again, not really hearing what he's saying at this point. "I don't need anyone. I have me. I have the angel."

"You have the—Helen, what the hell are you talking about."

"You're not worthy to gaze upon me," I say, kneeling to pick up my robe. "Your mortal eyes are not fit for my splendor." When I stand back up, the lightheadedness becomes so intense that my vision frays at the edges, curling into itself like burning paper, and I topple over onto my side. There should be pain, but there isn't. I have transcended pain. That, or the painkillers are still in full effect. I can't remember how long it's been since I took some. Hours, minutes. It doesn't matter.

Laughing from my place on the floor, I tell Jasper to get out. I tell him his services are no longer required. I tell him I'm so much better off without him.

"This isn't about us," he says. "You're, like...I think maybe you might be really sick, or something."

"Go fuck your fat girls," I tell him, still laughing. "This is what a real woman looks like, and you can't handle it. Do me a favor, though, and tell the front desk guy to stop sending visitors up without my permission. I don't want to deal with humans right now. They're beneath me."

"Um. Wow. Jesus Christ. You're just...like, you're so far gone."

"And *you're* not gone *enough*." My laughter has ceased. Now, all I feel is annoyance. "*Begone, peasant.* Looking at you is literally grossing me out."

He shakes his head, muttering "Jesus Christ" a few more times, and then he leaves. Once he's gone, the angel comes out of my bathroom and tells me I never needed him, that he was always holding me back.

"I know," I say. "I know."

The tears I'm crying are happy ones.

CHAPTER 25 – DRESSED IN DECAY

About six weeks into my sabbatical, I tell my agent I'm ready to start working again. Thrilled, he books me a Celine shoot with a British photographer I haven't worked with before. It's in a warehouse downtown, and apparently the other girls and I are going to be dressed as lingerie-clad mice. There will also be a boy dressed as a shirtless cat.

I'm feeling good when I arrive, even though I'm running late. My earphones are in, blaring "The Look" on repeat. I haven't consumed anything more than water in over sixty hours. The hunger euphoria is so intense I feel like I'm floating. I didn't even do any coke this morning. I didn't need it.

As I strut into the warehouse, pulling out my earphones and taking pleasure in the reverberatory echo of my heels, everyone turns to look at me. The boy is in his cat attire, and a few of the girls are already done up with whiskers and triangular ears and little gray noses. The girls pull into a tight cluster and begin whispering to each other. Their eyes never leave me. Some of them gape. The boy looks at me for a few moments, and then looks away.

I can't help but smile. The jealousy radiates from them.

The photographer appears with a woman in tow—a moderately attractive brunette in a blazer and a pencil skirt, carrying a ream of folders. The photographer's eyes land on me, and he frowns. He takes his Givenchy sunglasses off. Squinting, he advances a few steps in my

113

direction, and then stops. Turning to the woman in the skirt, he shouts, "Jesus fucking *Christ*, Vanessa. I fucking *told* you to stop *sending* me girls like this. For *fuck's sake.*" He looks at me again. "Bloody goddamn *hell.* Just fucking *look* at her. What the fuck were you *thinking?*"

"I...I didn't know she...I don't even know who she *is*," the woman sputters, rifling through her folders. To me, she says, "Um, could you give me your name, please?"

With brazen pride, I straighten and say, "My name is Helen Troy." I'm a little confused about the photographer's animosity, but I'm not sweating it. I feel too good to get worried about something so trivial. Photographers are temperamental, anyway.

"Ah," the woman says, pulling a headshot from one of the folders. "Here she is." She hands the picture to the photographer. "She doesn't look like that in her headshot," she murmurs.

Looking from me to the picture in his hands, the photographer says, "Fucking hell. When was this taken?"

"I had my headshots redone about a year ago," I say.

Coming closer and looking me up and down, he says, "Right then. Tell me, what do you think the theme of this shoot is?"

"Cat and Mouse?" I say, more confused.

"That's fucking right. Cat and Mouse. It's *not* fucking *Schindler's List.* So how about you fucking tell me why you showed up here looking like you just got off the last train out of fucking Auschwitz?"

I take off my huge Dita sunglasses—the Narcissus model; one of my favorite pairs—and perch them atop my head. I stare passively at the photographer for a moment, and then I look at the girls. I'm startled to realize that the perfect girl is among them. The one who sent me into my tailspin months ago. Except...she's *not* perfect. Not like I am. She's not as beautiful as I am, and certainly not as thin as I am. None of them are. Compared to me, they look like bloated beasts. Something so much less than human.

Nodding, I turn my attention back to the photo-

114

grapher. "Oh," I say. "I see what's going on here."

"Really? Do you? Because I don't fucking think you do."

"No, really. I get it." I put my sunglasses back on. "It all makes sense. You can't have me here among these girls. It's not fair. I make them look like dogs. And dogs don't have any place in a shoot with a Cat and Mouse theme." Some of the girls gasp, clapping hands to their mouths. The one I'd thought was perfect remains expressionless. It shocks me that she'd had so much power over me. That she could have triggered such sensations of inferiority. There's nothing special about her. She's looking at me now, and she's wishing she were me.

The photographer clenches his jaw. "You fucking well better listen here, young la—"

"No, *you* listen. You have two options. Either dismiss the rest of these ogres and do the shoot with me, *just* me, or watch me walk out of here and leave you with your Ugly Bitches R Us shitshow of a production."

"My God," he says, putting a hand to his forehead. "You're fucking delusional. You're actually legitimately fucking insane." He shakes his head, his eyes wide. "My God," he says again.

"God?" I scoff. "No. I'm the only god there is. And this—" I gesture around the warehouse "—all of *this* is beneath me, honestly. *You're* beneath me. Those girls are beneath me. Cat Man over there *wishes* he were beneath me, but he'll never fuck a girl *half* as hot as I am."

"I think you should go," the woman in the pencil skirt says.

"Honey," I say, "I'm already gone."

Shivering outside, smoking a cigarette as I'm waiting for my Lyft, I feel a hand on my shoulder. Turning, I'm faced with the girl I'd thought was perfect. She's wrapped in a kimono, and her face is contorted in an expression I can't at once decipher. Raising my sunglasses, I scrutinize her face. Try to match it with a list of emotions and keep coming up blank. The closest match I come up with— absurd as this is, and made even more so by the mouse getup—is pity. But that's not quite right, either. It's close, but not all the way there.

And then, it hits me.

It's sympathy. She looks sympathetic.

"Listen," she says, pulling the kimono tighter around her body. "I know you're not really in any place to hear this right now, but...I get it. I've been where you are. I know what it's like. I still struggle, obviously. I'm not all the way recovered, or anything. But I'm getting there. And I...look, I want to help. Someone helped me and it saved my life." She takes my hand and presses a slip of paper into my palm. There's a phone number written on it. "When it gets to be too much and you can't take it anymore, or even if you just want to talk...please, call me. Okay? There is a way out." She gives me a sad smile, squeezes my hand, and then goes back inside.

My phone vibrates. Turning back toward the street, I see my Lyft waiting at the curb. When I climb into the back seat, I crumple the slip of paper with the phone number on it and leave it in the gutter.

CHAPTER 26 – AN EPILOGUE OF YOUTH

I don't know how long it's been. Weeks, months—it doesn't make a difference; time has become irrelevant. All that matters now is being thinner.

MAKE YOURSELF FLAWLESS.

This is my beacon. My guiding light.

The angel tells me I'm almost there. She's with me all the time. She's the only person I see, and I like it that way. She's the only one who's worthy. I'm almost as thin as she is, but I'm still not quite there yet. She says I need to keep pushing. Keep restricting. That soon I'll not only equal her beauty but surpass it. I have to rely on what she tells me because I don't have a reflection anymore. When I look in the mirror, there's no one there. It's just empty glass. This was jarring at first, and more than a little disappointing, but I've come not only to accept my lack of reflection but appreciate it. I've always wanted to disappear.

I've lost control of my bladder, and the angel says this is because divine entities should not deign to such human trivialities as toilet use. I don't really defecate anymore, save for the occasional bloody mucus that runs down the backs of my near-perfect legs and leaves spots on the carpet. It is no matter. The angel doesn't mind, and she's the only company I keep.

My hair is falling out in clumps, too. It's scattered in ratty knots around my apartment, but the angel says it's being replaced by flame. Brilliant, glorious flame that cascades all around my head. The halo, she says, will be next.

The percussive thrumming sound never goes away, but I've grown to love it. It's like music. There are some nights when I become so enamored with its rhythms that I'm unable to resist the urge to dance to it. The angel joins me, and together we sway in the dim light of my apartment, or on the balcony with the glowing city miles beneath us, like gods in heaven.

For that's what we are, and what this is.

We are gods.

I am a god.

And I am in heaven.

I am happier than ever.

ACKNOWLEDGMENTS

I want to thank Autumn Christian, Sadie Hartmann, Joe Sullivan, Christina Pfeiffer, Marian Echevarria, JP, Gigi Levangie, Kelley Harron, Tracy Applegate, and Ryan Harding. There aren't enough words for my gratitude, so I won't try to come up with them.

Author photo by Mark Maryanovich

Chandler Morrison is the author of *Human-Shaped Fiends*, *Along the Path of Torment*, *Dead Inside*, *Until the Sun*, *Hate to Feel*, and *Just to See Hell*. His short fiction has appeared in numerous anthologies and literary journals. He lives in Los Angeles.

Printed in Great Britain
by Amazon

33439399R00070